Seven-Day Magic

Seven-Day Magic

Edward Eager

ILLUSTRATED BY N. M. BODECKER

SCHOLASTIC INC.

New York Toronto London Auckland Sydney
Mexico City New Delhi Hong Kong Buenos Aires

ISBN 0-439-32549-8

Copyright © 1962 by Edward Eager.
Copyright renewed 1990 by Jane Eager, Torsten Weld Bodecker,
Niels Weld Bodecker, Alexander Weld Bodecker.
All rights reserved.
Published by Scholastic Inc., 555 Broadway, New York, NY 10012,
by arrangement with Harcourt, Inc.
SCHOLASTIC and associated logos are trademarks and/or
registered trademarks of Scholastic Inc.

12 11 10 9 8 7 6   2 3 4 5 6/0

Printed in the U.S.A.   40

First Scholastic printing, September 2001

*For Ann Drakeley,
when she isn't quite so new,
and Peter Saxon,
if he hasn't grown too old*

CONTENTS

Seven-Day Magic

1

Finding It

"The best kind of book," said Barnaby, "is a magic book."

"Naturally," said John.

There was a silence, as they all thought about this and how true it was.

"The best kind of magic book," said Barnaby, leaning back against the edge of the long, low library table and surveying the crowded bookshelves, only seeming somehow to look beyond them and beyond everything else, too, the way he so often did, "is when it's about ordinary people like us, and then something happens and it's magic."

"Like when you find a nickel, except it isn't a nickel—it's a half-magic talisman," said Susan.

"Or you're playing in the front yard and somebody asks is this the road to Butterfield," said Abbie.

"Only it isn't at all—it's the road to Oz!" shrilled

Fredericka, jigging up and down excitedly, for she had read the book in which this happens.

The lady sitting at the far end of the table sighed and looked up, putting her hand to her head as if it ached. "Please," she said. "Can't we have quiet?"

"Now, now!" Miss Dowitcher, the librarian, wagged a finger in merry reproof as she skimmed past. "Now, now. This is a children's room, you know. It's for the children to enjoy."

The lady sighed again, closed the book she was reading, and opened another. Abbie tried to catch her eye and look sympathetic, but the lady would not meet her gaze.

Abbie knew the lady well, by sight. She was called Miss Prang, Miss Eulalie Smythe Prang, and she spent most of her days in the children's room at the library, looking in the different books and taking things out. When she had taken enough out, she put it together into a new book. There were a lot of her books on the library's shelves already, but they were not the kind of magic books Barnaby and John and Susan and Abbie and Fredericka had in mind. Mostly they were about dear little fairies who lived in buttercups.

Abbie sometimes thought that if Miss Prang would listen when she heard children talking, instead of sighing and putting her hand to her head, it might do her books a lot of good. For instance, she ought to be listening to Barnaby right now.

"The best kind of magic book," Barnaby was saying, "is the kind where the magic has rules. And you have to deal with it and thwart it before it thwarts you. Only sometimes you forget and get thwarted."

Everybody began talking at the same time, and the name of E. Nesbit was heard in more than one voice, for she was the five children's favorite author and no wonder (though Fredericka liked the Oz books nearly as well).

"Why couldn't she have lived forever?" said Abbie, taking that best of all Nesbit books, *The Enchanted Castle*, down from the shelf and looking at it with loving eyes. "We've read all of hers, and nobody seems to do books like that anymore."

"If you could have a brand-new magic book, specially made for you," said John, "what would you choose?"

"One about a lot of children," said Abbie.

"One about five children just like us," said Fredericka.

"And they're walking home from somewhere and the magic starts suddenly before they know it," said Susan.

"And they have to learn its rules and tame it and make the most of it," said Barnaby.

At the far end of the table Miss Prang muttered to herself, pushed the books about in front of her, and at last half rose to her feet, gazing imploringly in the direction of the librarian's desk.

Miss Dowitcher came skimming across the room again. "I think, then, children, if you're ready to go?" she murmured apologetically. "Perhaps it would be best. Have you found enough books to take?"

Of course they had not, for who has ever found enough books?

But they scrabbled together the ones they had chosen and lined up at the desk to have the date stamped in them. It was then that Susan looked back and saw the book sitting all by itself at one end of the bottom shelf.

It was a red book, smallish but plump, comfortable and shabby. There had once been gilt letters on the back, but these had rubbed away, and Susan couldn't read the name of what it was. Still, it looked odd enough to be interesting and worn enough to have been enjoyed by countless generations. On a sudden impulse she added it to the pile in her arms and took her place at the end of the line.

She thought Miss Dowitcher looked at her a bit strangely when she saw the red book, but "That's a seven-day book" was all she said. Susan was surprised. Usually the books that had to be returned in seven days were the newest ones, and new was the last thing she would have thought this book to be.

"Oh, we'll be through with it before that," she said.

"I wouldn't be too sure," remarked Miss Dowitcher, in rather a peculiar voice Susan thought. But she stamped the book with a will, and a minute later Susan and the others emerged from the library into the bright, new-washed June morning.

If you had seen the five children coming down the library steps that day, you would have thought they belonged to two families, and this was true.

John and Susan were tall and light-haired and calm. Barnaby and Abbie and Fredericka were little and quick and dark.

"You two look just the way you are," Barnaby had said one day, back when the two families had first met. "You look worthy and dependable. You look like people who would be president and vice president of the class."

"Well," admitted Susan apologetically, "we usually are."

She and John were president and vice president of the fifth grade this year. They were in the same class, not because they were twins (which they weren't) but because John had been very sick once and missed a whole year of school. But that was long ago.

Now John was big and strong and played quarterback on the school football team. Susan was captain of girls' soccer, and they were both rather good at chess. In schoolwork their marks generally averaged B, or at least B minus. Almost everybody liked them, even teachers, and their days were pleasant if uneventful.

Or at least that was the way things had always been up till last summer.

But then last summer Barnaby moved into the house across the road and turned out to be in their room in school, and after that things were changed.

Barnaby was a person with ideas.

"I don't see what you see in that little runt," big Pete Schroeder said to John at football practice one day back in the fall, when Barnaby was still the new boy in Miss Dugdale's room. "I don't see what you want to go round with him all the time for."

"It's like this," John told him. "He has ideas. And he's my best friend. So lay off."

Big Pete Schroeder laid off. Because John's word was law in five-one-A. The only one who could tell John what to do was Barnaby. Barnaby had ideas.

The ideas Barnaby had weren't always good ones,

but he had them one after another, all day long. And some of them were exciting.

He believed in magic, for one thing, or said he did. He believed that anything could happen, any minute, and that sometimes you could *make* things happen, if you tried hard enough. And he could think up wonderful games and ways to make the most boring things seem like fun.

Nobody would ever have taken Barnaby for the president of anything. He was not dignified enough. And everybody did not like him as much as John and Susan did. He was stubborn and hot-tempered and impatient, and when he disagreed with people, he started arguments. Miss Dugdale said the trouble with Barnaby was he was opinionated.

Susan sometimes tried to reason with Barnaby for his own good. And other times John had to step in and defend him when he got into fights with boys who were bigger than he was.

That was one thing about Barnaby, even his enemies agreed. He had spunk. He wasn't afraid of anybody. But he wasn't really at his best with his fists. He was more of a brain.

It was typical of him, Susan and John felt, to have an interesting and unusual name and to have sisters with interesting names, too, Abigail and Fredericka.

"*Our* names sound just like us," Susan complained one day after Barnaby had come into their lives.

"Good old Susan and John," agreed John.

Barnaby liked his own name. He was proud of its differentness and would never answer to "Barney" or any other nickname. And Fredericka was just the same. People took their lives in their hands who dared to call her "Freddy." Fredericka was the baby of the family and even fiercer-tempered than Barnaby.

But everybody called Abigail Abbie.

Abbie was that kind of person, just jolly and friendly, with no temper at all. Barnaby always said Abbie must be a throwback, only he couldn't decide what she was a throwback *to*. She wasn't a bit like the rest of the family.

"That's 'cause she's the middle one," said Barnaby's father, overhearing this one afternoon. "Middle ones are mild. Only don't count on it. She may surprise you someday." He ruffled Abbie's hair, and Abbie gave him a loving look.

Barnaby and Abbie and Fredericka's father was a nice man. He was a singer on television, but not a famous one yet. Mostly you saw him as one of a quartet singing that his beer was Finegold, the dry beer, or wanting someone to be sociable and have a Poopsi.

He was little and quick and dark like Barnaby, and when he was at home playing croquet or badminton with the kids, he looked more like their brother than their father. But he wasn't home so very often, because with three children to support, he had to go in to New York at all kinds of hours on all kinds of different singing jobs.

Barnaby's mother used to be a dancer, but now she went whizzing around all day in her old car, trying to sell other people houses, to help make ends meet and keep up their payments on their own house. Their house was new and little, just large enough to hold a family of five.

Susan and John's house across the road was big and old. Sometimes Susan thought it was *too* big for just her and John and Grannie.

Susan and John's parents had died a long time ago, the same year John was so sick. After that Grannie came to stay with them, but whether she was taking care of them or they were taking care of her was never quite clear. Susan and John often felt as if Grannie were the child and they were the grownups. Grannie was like that.

She was little and frail and older than most

grandmothers and yet almost too energetic. And she was so unexpected in what she might do and often did, such as climbing cherry trees or shoveling snow off the walk, that Susan and John hated to leave her alone in the house any more than they had to. Sometimes one of them would miss a party sooner than have both of them go out for a whole evening at the same time.

Not that Grannie would have climbed trees or shoveled snow in the dark of night, but she would probably think of something just as dangerous and unsuitable.

So altogether it was wonderful for Susan and John when Barnaby moved into the little new house and they had a friend right at home, almost in the front yard.

And then to have the friend turn out to be a person with ideas was almost too good to be true.

One of the ideas Barnaby had was that Susan and John should get acquainted with the public library. Up till then John hardly read anything at all, outside of school. And Susan mostly read about Sue Barton, student nurse.

But books were Barnaby's life blood, maybe because he was an author himself. He had a book of his own in his mind, and some of it down on paper, but he would never talk about it or tell the others what it was.

Except that he had told a little of it to Abbie, for she was a poet, or hoped to be, and would understand.

Most of the time when Barnaby wasn't having ideas or thinking about his own book, he was reading other people's. He read one a day, at *least*, and was anxious that his friends should do the same. It was Barnaby who had decided that Saturday was library day.

Each Saturday morning, as soon as breakfast was over, the five children would ride along with Barnaby's mother on her way to the office (and with Barnaby's father, too, if he were catching the train for an early rehearsal) and get off at the library corner.

Later, after an hour or two of rummaging and browsing (and a lot of advice from Barnaby), they would come down the library steps and walk along the village street that turned into the curving country road home, reading as they went. And Barnaby had made a game of that, too. Each one got to read part of his most interesting-looking book out loud, and then the others were free to criticize.

This particular June morning started out no differently from the others. As the five children wandered along Cherry Street, Barnaby opened his top book hopefully and began chapter one. But after only a paragraph or two he leafed over to the back, glanced at the last pages, and shut the cover with a disgusted bang.

"I thought so," he said. "Of all the gyps! It calls itself *The Magic Door*, but there's not a speck of real magic in it anywhere! It's just about this boy that learns to get along with these other people by being friendly and stuff. And the magic door's just the door of good fellowship or something. Man, do I despise a book like that!"

And the others could not have agreed with him more. Usually the five children could spot a book like that a mile off, though. It wasn't very often that they got fooled.

So then, of course, Fredericka had to read about Ozma's birthday party from the end of *The Road to Oz*, the way she almost always did. The others never minded listening to this once again. It took them back to their own happy, carefree, innocent childhood.

When she had finished, Barnaby looked around at the others. "Anybody else?"

Ordinarily Susan would have been the last to answer. She wasn't a quick reader out loud and was afraid of disgracing herself in Barnaby's hearing by stumbling over long words. But today she looked at the little old shabby-looking book on the top of her pile, and something made her change her mind.

"I've got this book here," she said.

"What is it?" said Barnaby. "Who's it by?"

"I don't know," said Susan. "It doesn't seem to say. I just kind of think it might be interesting." And she opened the worn red cover and began to read.

These are the words that Susan read:

" 'The best kind of book,' said Barnaby, 'is a magic book.'

'Naturally,' said John.

'The best kind of magic book,' said Barnaby, leaning back against the edge of the long, low library table and surveying the crowded bookshelves, only seeming somehow to look beyond them and beyond everything else, too, the way he so often did, 'is when it's about ordinary people like us, and then something happens and it's magic.'

'Like when you find a nickel, except it isn't a nickel—it's a half-magic talisman,' said Susan.

'Or you're playing in the front yard and some-body asks is this the road to Butterfield,' said Abbie.

'Only it isn't at all—it's the road to Oz!' shrilled Fredericka, jigging up and down excitedly . . ."

Susan's voice trailed off. She looked at the others.

"It can't be," said Barnaby.

"It is," said Susan. "It's about *us*! All of us, and every single thing we said!"

"Let's see."

Barnaby reached for the book, rather greedily Susan thought, and yet what of it? This was no time to be worrying about manners, and Barnaby could read the fastest. He was reading fast now, flipping over the pages one after the other.

"You're right," he muttered as he read. "We're all in it."

"How could we be?" said John. "How'd we get there without our knowing it?"

"I don't know," said Barnaby, "but we're there all right. It tells about us, and our parents, and your Grannie, even. And a lot more about me being stubborn and unpopular and you sticking up for me," he went on, his face getting rather red.

"What does it say about *me*?" said Fredericka.

"It says you're fierce-tempered," said Barnaby.

"Well, I am," said Fredericka.

There was a silence. Everybody stopped walking and just stood there.

"What's happening?" said Abbie. "Do you suppose we're magic, suddenly?"

"Either we are," said John, "or that book is."

"Maybe it isn't a book at all," said Fredericka in eerie tones.

"I don't like it," said Abbie. "It's creepy. Let's take it back and tell the library we don't want it."

"Or bury it with a stake through its heart," said Barnaby.

But nobody laughed.

"Do you suppose," said Susan, "we're not really real at all but just characters in this book somebody wrote?"

This was a sobering thought.

"I don't *want* to be not real," said Fredericka, all of a sudden not seeming fierce-tempered at all but just little and scared.

There was another silence. Everybody looked at Barnaby. Barnaby thought a minute. Then he shook his head.

"No," he said, "it can't be that. Because when the book tells about me and Abbie and Fredericka, it says we've just moved here. But I remember being me long before that."

"Maybe that part of you was in *another* book," said Susan. She didn't mean to say it, but it just slipped out.

Barnaby was undaunted. "All right," he said. "Suppose we *are* book characters? It never bothered us before, before we thought about it. It doesn't have to bother us now. Characters have all kinds of interesting things happen to them. And here's a whole bookful of adventures and we're just at the beginning!"

"What happens next?" said Fredericka, standing on tiptoe and trying to see over Barnaby's shoulder (only she was too little to reach).

"What happens at the *end*?" said Abbie. "That's what *I'm* worrying about!"

"How far did you get?" said Susan. "Did the Susan in the book find an old book in the library, too, and start reading out loud from it?"

"That's where I stopped," said Barnaby. " 'Susan opened the worn red cover and began to read,' it says."

"Just think," John said dreamily. "If we find a book about people like us and the people *in* the book find a book about people like *them*, and the people in *that* book find a book about people like . . ."

"Don't!" cried Susan. "It's like those awful arithmetic problems that go on and on." She turned back to Barnaby. "*Then* what does the book say. Is it taking down everything we're saying now, like a stenographer?"

"No," said Barnaby. "It doesn't say *anything* then. The page ends there."

"Turn over," said Fredericka.

"Look in the back," said Abbie.

Barnaby tried. "I can't," he told them. "It's stuck or something. The whole rest of the book's shut solid tight."

"I suppose that's as much as they want us to know," said Abbie darkly. "And now I suppose the awful thing happens."

"What awful thing?" said Fredericka.

"I don't know. Some awful thing. It stands to reason."

"Not necessarily," said Barnaby. And then even he broke off and caught his breath and looked around warily.

But what happened was nothing at all. Except that the sun went on shining and the sky went on being blue and some cars drove by and an oriole sang and a woman came out of a house and began beating a carpet.

After a few minutes of this usualness everyone found himself breathing more regularly again. The five children found themselves walking along again, too, and waiting for Barnaby to begin having more ideas. And pretty soon he did.

"Of course," he said. "I'm beginning to see it all. Don't you remember? We said we wanted a special magic book of our own."

"About five children just like us," said Abbie. "*You* said that part." And she pointed an accusing finger at Fredericka.

"No matter who said what," said Barnaby, "it looks as if we got it, somehow. But *something* had to make the wish come true. And what else but the book itself could have done that?" He turned to Susan. "Where'd you find it in the first place?"

"On the bottom shelf of the fairy-tale section," she said, remembering.

Barnaby nodded excitedly. "It all adds up. Think of it sitting there all those years, with the magic from all those other books dripping down onto it! It's prob'ly *soaked* with magic powers by now. It's prob'ly been sitting there waiting for somebody to come along and make a wish in front of it. And we came and wanted a magic story; so that's what it turned into. Prob'ly if we'd wanted pirates, it'd have turned into a book about a pirate ship with us on board. But we asked for magic; so that's what we got."

"What kind of wish is that?" said Fredericka. "What good is a book about us? We *know* about us."

"We don't know what's coming next," said Barnaby. "All we've had is the beginning. What else did we wish for? Think back."

"I said the people in the book would be walking

1 9

home from somewhere and the magic would start suddenly before they knew it," said Susan.

"Well?" said Barnaby. "*That* part came true. And then *I* said they'd have to tame the magic and learn its rules and thwart it and make the most of it. So I guess it's up to us to do that from now on."

Barnaby was certainly having ideas today. In fact, he was having them so fast the others could hardly keep up with him. But they were exciting ideas, all the same.

"You mean," said Susan, "there's a whole book still going to happen to us?"

"That's what I think," said Barnaby.

"But if it's all there in the book," said John, "why not use the magic and wish the book open? So we can read the next chapter and know what to expect?"

"I don't think it works like that," said Barnaby. "I think that'd be against the rules. Anyway, maybe there *isn't* any next chapter, yet. I think if we could pry open the rest of the pages, they'd prob'ly be blank. I think it's prob'ly up to us to make more wishes and have them come true, so as to fill the pages up!"

"Sort of make up the book as we go along?" said Abbie.

"You mean it's ours to *use*?" said Susan. "Like a wishing ring, sort of?"

"Only mixed up with those things they have in offices," said Fredericka. "Those things you talk into."

"Dictaphones," said John.

"Whatever they're called," said Fredericka.

"That's the idea," said Barnaby. "More or less."

Everyone thought about this.

"That book," said John, "had better be handled with care from now on."

"Don't anybody dare even *think* about wishing," said Susan, "till we've talked it out and decided what kind of adventure we want."

"*You* ought to do the deciding," said Barnaby. "You're the one who found the book in the first place."

That was typical of Barnaby. He might be grabby, but he was fair. Susan's hand went out toward the book. Then she pulled it back and shook her head. Barnaby was the one with ideas. Let him go on having them.

"No, you go first. You'll do it better."

"No, *you* ought to be the one."

"No, honestly, I'd rather."

"Oh, for heaven's sake," said Fredericka. "If

everybody else is too polite around here, let *me*!"
And she laid hold of the book.

"Stop her, somebody!" cried Abbie. But it was too late. Fredericka was already talking, gabbling her words without stopping to breathe for fear someone would interrupt her, the way youngest children in families soon learn to do.

"I wish we'd have a magic adventure, with wizards and witches and magic things in it, and I wish it'd start right now, this minute, so we'll know for certain it's really our wish coming true and not just a coincidence!"

"That's done it," said Barnaby, when Fredericka finally stopped just before utter breath failed.

But it didn't seem to have. Nothing happened.

"Maybe the book didn't hear her," said Abbie.

"Maybe I'm supposed to kiss it or something," said Fredericka.

"Maybe we're supposed to keep on walking," said Barnaby. "The minute isn't up yet."

They kept on walking. Round a bend in the road they came on a house they had always specially noticed in the past. It was a perfectly ordinary-looking house in a perfectly ordinary-looking garden, but it had an interesting sign by the driveway.

"Slow," warned the sign. "Cats, et cetera."

In the past the five children had often stopped

and waited by the driveway, in hope that something other than a cat would come out. But up till this second nothing had.

At this second (which happened to be the fifty-ninth since Fredericka had made her wish), something did.

What came out was a dragon.

2

Using It

The dragon was bright red all over, except for its eyes, which were green. It was flying low over the driveway, puffing purple smoke as it came.

Abbie stopped short and clutched the others. But Fredericka pressed forward curiously. And the dragon seemed just as curious as Fredericka. It hovered over her in hawklike circles, peering down. For a moment their eyes met. Then it scooped her up in its scaly grasp and flew away with her, over the trees.

"Stop!" cried John, starting to run in the direction it had taken.

"Do something!" cried Abbie, pulling at Barnaby. "Use the book! Wish!" She turned to Susan.

"Wait," said Barnaby. He was as pale as the others, but he was having ideas, all the same. "You'll never find it that way," he called to John. "It's prob'ly over some other county by now."

John stopped running, for indeed the dragon

(and Fredericka) had disappeared in the far distance, and the last puff of purple smoke was merging into the clouds.

"And let's not make any more wishes without stopping to think," Barnaby went on. "Fredericka did that, and look what happened! But she asked for a magic adventure and this is it. I think we ought to start by finding out whose dragon it *is*."

"Look!" said Susan, pointing up the driveway.

A ground-floor window of the house was open, and a face was staring out at the four children. The face wore a surprised expression.

Abbie, usually so timid, ran right across the lawn and up to the face, and the others followed.

"Was that your dragon?" she demanded sternly.

"Oh dear," said the face. "Is *that* what it was? I was *afraid* that was what it was!"

"Well, you ought to be more careful!" Abbie scolded. "You let it get away, and now it's stolen my little sister!"

"Oh dear," said the face again. "I *am* sorry."

Now that they were near, the four children could see that the face belonged to a little round gentleman with a bald head. He wore an old-fashioned long coat, a fancy vest, and a flowing tie. In his hand was a tall silk hat, which he was regarding in a distracted manner.

"I don't know what can have gone wrong," he went on. "Such a thing never happened before. I was practicing my tricks the way I always do after breakfast, and I reached into my hat to pull out a rabbit, and *something* came out, only it was something *else!*"

"It certainly *was!*" said John.

"I could tell it wasn't a rabbit," said the round gentleman, "from the feel. But I didn't dare to look. Then it went whoosh, and it was gone."

Barnaby turned to the others. "You can see what prob'ly happened. Fredericka prob'ly made her wish at that exact minute, and that prob'ly did it."

The round gentleman did not appear to have heard this. "I'm sorry to have inconvenienced any sister of yours," he went on. "Still, it shows I haven't lost my knack, doesn't it?"

Barnaby looked at him. And he remembered the rest of Fredericka's wish. "You must be a wizard," he said.

The round gentleman looked pleased. "How did you guess? It is true that is my profession, though 'magician' is the proper term. In vaudeville they called me The Great Oswaldo."

"What's Vaudeville?" whispered Abbie to Barnaby.

"It's a kind of show they used to have, back before television," he whispered back.

"Oh," said Abbie. She had thought Vaudeville might be a magic kingdom, rather like Oz or Narnia. Still, at a time like this, even a stage wizard was probably better than no wizard at all. And the round gentleman appeared kind. So she said, "You'll help us, won't you? You'll find my sister for us?"

The round gentleman looked uncertain. "Well, I'll *try*," he said. "Won't you come in?" And he left the window.

"Shall we?" said Susan.

"Proceed as the door opens," said Barnaby.

But when the round gentleman opened the door of the house, the four children hesitated. The hall inside looked dark and spooky, and there were sounds, a furry flumping and a padding and a purring and a murmur of mews.

"Better not. He's got more wild beasts!" warned John.

"Merely a few household pets," said the round gentleman. "When I retired, I thought a cat would be company, but they mounted up." And he switched on the hall light.

The four children regarded the scene inside with interest. Cats wreathed about the round gentleman's feet, and the bottoms of his trousers were patterned with their paw prints. And the children knew now what the "et cetera" on the sign had stood for. The "et cetera" was kittens. They sat on the stair and stared through the banisters and played on the plate rail.

"Aw!" said Abbie, running to pick up the smallest and fluffiest kitten and hold it against her. And the other three followed her into the hall. As they did so, a woman appeared from the back of the house.

"Who are all these?" she said. "Feet on my good rugs. As if them cats weren't enough!"

"It's all right, Mrs. Funkhouser," said the round gentleman. "These visitors are for *me*. Mrs. Funkhouser is my landlady," he went on, when the woman had muttered herself away. "A good woman, but not much artistic temperament. And now if you'll step this way?"

He went through a door at the end of the hall, and the four children followed. When they saw the room beyond the door, Abbie's eyes grew wide with wonder, and John said, "Whew!"

The room looked very much as yours does when you have played with your Mysto-Magic set and forgotten to pick it up and then the cat has got in.

Only in this case it was more like twenty magic sets and thirty cats. Crystal balls and bottles of colored liquid and jars of colored powder and phials and retorts and spirit lamps were on every table and shelf. But most of the bottles were tipped over and most of the powder was spilled. Cats and kittens moved among the remains.

"I'm afraid we're a little untidy this morning," said the round gentleman. "I don't know what Mrs. Funkhouser would say."

The four children thought they knew what she would say all too well.

"However," the gentleman went on, looking at the litter of paraphernalia and fluttering his hands in rather a helpless way, "we'll see what we can do. I'm afraid I may be a bit rusty. It's years now since my farewell appearance. And I never found a lost girl, even in the old days. I'm not quite certain how it's done. I used to saw a lady in half at one time, but it's not quite the same thing."

"It certainly isn't!" said Susan indignantly.

"I might try the hat trick again and see what comes out *this* time," suggested the round gentleman.

But when he put his hand in the hat, what came out wasn't Fredericka or even a white rabbit. What came out was the smallest kitten, who had left Abbie's shoulder and crawled into the hat when no one was looking.

"Sorry," said the gentleman. "I suppose it would be more to the point to get the dragon back *into* the hat, wouldn't it? Or transform him to some more harmless form. Where's my box of tricks?" He found a card index and riffled through it. "Transformations," he muttered. "There's only one listed here, but as I remember, it was always colorful."

He found a blue handkerchief in the litter on the nearest table and drew it through a wooden ring.

The handkerchief was transformed from blue to red, but Fredericka did not return. And if the dragon (wherever it was by now) was altered in any way, it did not put in an appearance to make the fact known.

"You're not trying," said Abbie accusingly. She was beginning to suspect that the round gentleman might be a *good* wizard without being very good *at* it.

"Yes, I am," said the round gentleman. "The third time's always the one that works." His eyes roamed the room, rather desperately Susan thought. "There's *this*," he said, picking up a bottle of purple liquid, seemingly at random.

"What does it do?" said John.

"It's *supposed* to make a red flare," said the round gentleman, "but the way things have been going this morning, *anything* might happen!" And he emptied the bottle into a bowl.

As he did so, Susan had an idea.

She wasn't sure yet just how the magic of the book worked. It had already proved it could get them *into* adventures, but after that, did it just sit back and watch or would it help?

Who could say? Still, there was no harm in trying. And she felt sorry for the round gentleman and wanted to help him (to say nothing of Fredericka). So she held the book firmly in both hands and wished with all her might that this time the magic would prove successful.

The round gentleman struck a match and lit the fluid in the bowl. It made a red flare, all right. But other things happened, too. There was a whooshing noise, followed by a whirring one.

"It wasn't supposed to do *that*," said the round gentleman. "Or *that*, either," he added, as there was a sudden jolt, and everybody's stomach felt the way yours does when you're in an elevator and it starts going up too fast.

"We're moving," said Barnaby. "Flying, I *think*."

John ran to the window. "That's right, we're right

off the ground. We're heading the same way the dragon did, too!"

Two treetops passed by the window, going from left to right, just to prove it.

"Oh dear," said the round gentleman, turning pale. "What will Mrs. Funkhouser say? She always claims she runs a well-run house, but I don't think she'd want it to *fly*!"

What Mrs. Funkhouser would say was soon made clear.

"Mr. Oswaldo," she said, appearing sternly in the doorway, "you put this house down right this minute!"

The round gentleman shook his head. "I would if I could," he said, "but I can't. I don't know how."

"This," said Mrs. Funkhouser, "is the last straw. Mama always said never rent to theatricals or they'd raise the roof. If we ever get back to lower Weed Street, your room'll be wanted!"

"I'm sorry," said the round gentleman. But he didn't look sorry. He was smiling. "Still, it's a good trick, isn't it? I didn't know I had it in me!"

Susan said nothing. But she gave the book a grateful pat.

Barnaby saw her do it. Their eyes met, and he seemed to put two and two together. He nodded to himself. Then he turned to the round gentleman.

"You keep it up," he said kindly. "You're doing fine."

When the dragon first flew away with Fredericka, she thought her last hour had come. But as the minutes went by and it didn't actually bite, her hopes rose. Dragon stories in books sometimes had happy endings. Maybe a prince would come and rescue her. Or maybe Barnaby would.

By the time she dared to look down, the landscape beneath wasn't modern Connecticut any more. The country below had a long-ago, fairy-tale look. There were rings in the grass that could be fairy rings and caves in the mountains that might belong to gnomes.

"Where am I?" she murmured.

"In magic realms, of course," said the dragon, "and faery lands forlorn. That was what you wished for, wasn't it?"

Fredericka jumped (as well as she could in the dragon's grasp). She hadn't expected an answer. Then she took courage. If the dragon could talk, it was probably a superior type, perhaps even a friendly one. "How do wishes work, *exactly*?" she said. "I've always wanted to know."

"I don't know how they work for *you*," said the dragon, "but for us magic things they're sort of doorways into the real world. We'll always get in if we can. Only there aren't many doors left. You must have found one of the last."

"Oh," said Fredericka. She thought for a minute. "But if you wanted to get into *our* world, why didn't you stay there?"

"What's even better," said the dragon, "is to steal somebody out of your world into *ours*. The door works both ways. You've heard of fairies kidnaping children. It's the same with dragons. Only different."

Fredericka cleared her throat. "Different in what way?" she asked cautiously. "Where are you taking me?"

"To my lair, of course," said the dragon.

"Why?" said Fredericka.

The dragon appeared embarrassed. "For the usual purpose," it said finally. "Let's not talk about it."

"You mean . . . ?" said Fredericka.

"*You* know," said the dragon.

"Oh," said Fredericka, in a small voice.

There was a pause.

"Why?" said Fredericka. "Why are you so mean?"

"Made that way," said the dragon, shrugging its wings (and causing rather a bumpy downdraft).

"Have you ever thought," suggested Fredericka, "of going on a vegetable diet? Trees might be tasty."

The dragon shook its head. "Meat," it said, "is

meat and drink to me. Of course I prefer princess, but it's almost gone off the market lately. Damsel generally does as well. Or maiden. I've never tried small girl before, but it should be tender, from the feel." And it gripped her tighter in its steely claws.

Fredericka tried to square her jaw. "I'm *not*," she said. "I'm tough as *anything*!" And she made up her mind that she would *try* to be when the time came.

But in spite of herself, her lip trembled and her spirits faltered and her heart sank. She wondered where Barnaby and the others were, and if pretty soon they would wish on the book and everything would come out right, or if her own wish had foiled the book and the magic had gone out of it and she would never see her family and friends and the real world again.

And the dragon flew on.

Meanwhile, a few miles back, so did Mrs. Funkhouser's house. And now Abbie, at the window, was looking down on the same fairy-tale landscape Fredericka had observed a few minutes before.

"What country *is* it, do you suppose?" she said. "It can't be Oz, or it'd be all blue or yellow or red or purple or with emeralds."

"I don't care for the look of it," said Mrs. Funk-

houser, joining her at the window. "It's not a con-
venient neighborhood. There's no supermarket. I
want to go home."

"It's too late," said Barnaby, peering over their
shoulders. "We're landing."

The meadows and caves were suddenly rushing
nearer, and a crowd of people could be seen below,
staring upwards.

John joined the watchers at the window. Susan
and the round gentleman hung back, but a second
later they went sliding along the floor. The combined
weight of the others proved too much for the house's
balance, and it slowly tilted, then tipped forward
on its face. All the people fell on top of all the *other*
people, and all the cats and kittens fell furrily and
fussily and waulingly and scratchingly on top of
them. The smallest kitten would have fallen right
through the window, but Barnaby caught it in time.

"Everybody back!" he cried. "Distribute your
weight or we'll crash!"

The others climbed up the slanty floor and placed
themselves about the room till the house righted
itself, and not a second too soon. There was a slight
jar. Then all was still, but only for a moment. Following the jar came a roaring sound from without.

"The dragon!" cried Abbie in alarm.

"No," said Barnaby. "It's people, and I think they're cheering."

"Come on," said John. And he and Barnaby and Susan and Abbie and the round gentleman made their way out of the house.

Outside was a primrosey meadow, with an old-fashioned-looking village in the background. A crowd of peasants stood nearby. You could tell they were peasants by their peasant costumes. When they spoke, they spoke peasant, too.

"Hooray, hooray!" they said. "Be you come to kill the dragon and save us all?"

"Why, yes," said Barnaby. "At least I hope so."

The leader of the peasants came nearer and looked them over. "Well," he said, "leastways you be a change. Mostly we get princes. Mostly they come by horse, not house. Mostly they don't kill it, neither. Mostly they get et."

"*We* won't," said Abbie, hoping that she spoke the truth. "We brought our magic. We brought a wizard, too!"

"Magician, please," corrected the round gentleman.

The first peasant looked at him. Then he looked beyond him. "You'm brought a witch, too, seems like."

The four children followed his gaze. Mrs. Funk-houser was just emerging from the house. So were the cats. But the cats' nerves had been rudely shocked by the tilting and tipping of the house, and they were still arching their backs and hissing. Some of the more maddened ones were climbing up Mrs. Funkhouser's dress and clawing at her hair. To say that as a group they presented a witchlike aspect would be putting it mildly.

But Mrs. Funkhouser had heard the peasant's comment and resented it. "I," she told him, "am a respectable woman."

The peasant nodded. "Good," he said. "You be a *good* witch, then. That's the best kind."

"And now," said Barnaby, trying to sound more courageous than he felt, "lead us to your dragon."

"It be right there," said the peasant.

"Where?" said all four children, jumping.

"There, in the lair," said the peasant, pointing.

The four children looked where he pointed. Beyond the house was a cave in the rock that they hadn't noticed before. A huffing sound of breathing came from within, and with each huff a puff of purple smoke issued from the cavern's mouth.

"He sounds awfully *relaxed*," said Susan. "Do you suppose he's eaten her already?"

"No," said the first peasant, "he hain't. He feeds prompt at noon. 'Tis the custom."

"Mornings he goes a-hunting," said a second peasant. "All among the local maidens. 'Tis a curse on us."

"One a day he eats," said a third, "till the hero comes who'll kill the beast and rule the country. 'Tis the prophecy."

"Not many maidens left by now," said a fourth peasant. "Seems like the race may die out afore *he* does. 'Tis a problem."

"Today's maiden makes no never-minds, though," said a fifth. "'Tis a stranger."

"Nobody we know," agreed a sixth.

"So *that's* all right," said the seventh (and last) peasant.

Abbie turned on the crowd of peasants indignantly. "It is *not* all right!" she cried. "She is *not* a stranger! She's my little sister!" And before Barnaby could stop her, she ran to the mouth of the cave. "Fredericka!" she called wildly.

Within the lair Fredericka heard her sister's voice and struggled in the dragon's grip. "Help!" she called back.

"Hush now," said the dragon fussily, bending over her. "I never like it when folks scream. Spoils the taste going down and upsets my digestion, later."

"It *does*?" said Fredericka, considerably encouraged. And she screamed again, even louder.

"What a horrible sound! It must be eating her *now*!" cried Susan, holding her ears.

"No," said the first peasant, "it hain't. It feeds prompt at noon, and it feeds in public, to scarify us."

John looked at his watch. "It's three minutes to twelve," he said.

"We've got to do something fast," said Barnaby, turning to the round gentleman.

"Oh dear," said the round gentleman. "Now the time has come, I don't believe I *can*!"

But a new voice was heard. "Shame on you, Mr. Oswaldo," it said. "The one time your pesky magic might be some use, don't you *dare* back out!"

Everyone turned in surprise. It was Mrs. Funkhouser. Apparently beneath her cross exterior she had hidden depths, and Fredericka's cries had plumbed them.

"You save that little girl," she said now, "or take a week's notice from Tuesday!"

"Well, I'll *try*," said the round gentleman, "but I doubt if I'll be much help."

"Of course you will," said Susan encouragingly. "It stands to reason. The book wouldn't have brought you in, otherwise. Or you, either," she added, turning to Mrs. Funkhouser.

Mrs. Funkhouser gave her a sharp look. "What book would that be?"

Susan looked at Barnaby, and Barnaby gave a little nod. "Well, you see we have this magic book," said Susan.

"We're not sure yet just how it works," said John.

"But it more or less began the whole thing," said Barnaby.

"Let me see it," said Mrs. Funkhouser and the round gentleman, both speaking at once.

Susan started to answer. But at that moment the steeple bells in the nearby village chimed noon, and the dragon emerged from its lair. And her words were drowned in a gasp.

The children had had only a fleeting glimpse of the dragon before. Now as it paraded up and down, displaying itself to the crowd, they saw its scaly scarlet sides and its hideous hungry jaws and its calamitous wreathing tail, and their hearts sank.

"Don't just stand there. *Do* something!" Fredericka called to her friends and relations, from the dragon's grasp.

Susan roused herself. "I will," she said. And she handed the book to the round gentleman.

If you have understood about the book so far, you will know that for each person its power was different, because to each person it was the particular book that person had always longed to find.

So that while for the five children it was a magic story with them *in* it, for the round gentleman it was something else again.

" '*Wishful Ways for Wizards*!' " he read, from the title page. "Why, this is wonderful! If I'd had this when I was in vaudeville, I needn't have retired in the first place!" He turned the book's pages, sampling its contents. " 'How to Turn Day to Night,' 'How to Tell Chalk from Cheese,' 'One Hundred Easy Card Tricks'!" he read.

"Don't just *skim*! Find the right place!" called the captive Fredericka.

"To be sure," said the round gentleman shamefacedly. "I was forgetting. 'How to Shrink a Dragon.' I'm sure I saw it here somewhere. Now *where . . .* ?" He leafed through the pages.

"Oh, for pity's sake let *me*!" said Mrs. Funkhouser, taking the book from him. But of course once in her housewifely hands, the book was a book of another color.

" '*Helpful Hints for Homemakers*,' " she read. " 'You take your skillet . . .' "

The dragon, annoyed at this interruption, glared

in her direction, and its gaze fell upon the book's title.

"That isn't what it says," said the dragon. "It says, *'Dreadful Deeds for Dragons.'* And I want it!" It set Fredericka down, keeping one claw on her for safekeeping, and stretched its other claw toward Mrs. Funkhouser.

"Don't look at *me*, you nasty creature, don't!" said Mrs. Funkhouser, snatching the book away. "Oh, you would, would you?" she added, as the dragon shot out an angry tongue of flame and a cloud of smoke. She consulted the book. " 'To put out an oven fire, use salt,' " she read. "That ought to do it. Fetch the salt, somebody."

John ran into the house.

"Stop interfering," said the dragon. "Do I have to eat you, too? Oh, very well!" And it opened its cavernous mouth.

Then it hesitated. Mrs. Funkhouser looked as if she would be all gristle. Fredericka undoubtedly would prove more toothsome. Should he save her till last or eat her first, as an appetizer?

But he who hesitates is often lost.

While the dragon was making up its mind, John came running out of the house with the salt box, and Mrs. Funkhouser shook it full in the dragon's face.

There was a hissing sound, and the dragon's fire went out.

I have heard it said that when a dragon's fire is put out, the dragon is rendered harmless. This is not true. Because what *I* say is, what about the teeth? They would still be there, fire or no fire. In this case they were, and the dragon now showed all of them in a snarl of fury.

At the same time, having its fire put out hurts a dragon's pride and lowers it in its own esteem. And since a dragon's belief in itself is part of a dragon's power, it is lowered in the public eye, also. In this case by about ten feet. It had been a forty-foot dragon to start with; so the change made quite a difference.

The crowd cheered.

The dragon trembled with rage and frustration and snapped at Mrs. Funkhouser. But it was not yet used to its new size, and its coordination was poor. So was its aim.

"Bite *me*, would you?" said Mrs. Funkhouser, dodging it easily. She consulted the book again. " 'For bites, stings, et cetera, use household ammonia,' " she read.

Barnaby did not wait to be asked but went rushing into the house.

"This is undignified," said the dragon. "Either

get a sword and fight me properly, or withdraw from the combat!"

Mrs. Funkhouser did not deign to answer. Barnaby was back by now with the bottle from under the sink, and she took it from him and emptied it in the general direction of the dragon.

The dragon sneezed and sputtered and coughed. Otherwise, it was not physically hurt. Its hurt went deeper. To be salted and ammoniaed by a domestic housewife is humiliating to a dragon and makes it feel small.

And when a dragon feels small, it *is*.

Small, however, is a relative term, which means that it can mean many things. A small lion is bigger than a large flea.

As for a small dragon, it is about the size of a large dog. And such now proved to be the case.

The crowd cheered again.

"This is monstrous," said the dragon, looking over its shoulder to see what size it was *this* time. "You are breaking *all* the rules. St. George would have shown more consideration!"

"My turn now!" cried the round gentleman, dancing up and down with impatience and trying to catch a look at the book. " 'To Shrink a Dragon'— I know I saw it somewhere . . ."

But the next turn proved to be the cats'.

When the dragon had first come out of its lair, all the cats and kittens had hidden behind Mrs. Funkhouser's skirts. Now, as the fumes from the ammonia reached their sensitive nostrils, they said "Pig-whiff!", put back their ears, and peered out.

What they saw seemed to be a large (and unusually ugly) dog at bay. As such, it was fair game for taunting. The cats had already had an extremely nerve-wracking morning, and they were in no gentle mood.

They stalked forth, lashing their tails.

You may have heard that an elephant is afraid of a mouse. With dragons and cats it is very much the same. I think it has to do with claws and scales. The one might so easily scratch off the other. You may have noticed your own cat with your mother's nylon stockings. It is the same principle.

The dragon saw the cats coming and shrank in fear. And once it started shrinking, it couldn't seem to stop.

It shrank from the size of a large collie to the size of a medium-sized poodle. The cats stood around it in a circle, glaring and spitting. The dragon took one look at them and shrank in fear again.

It shrank to the size of a small Pekingese, and the cats and kittens approached it and rattled their claws against its sides.

"This is unendurable," said the dragon. "You tickle."

It shrank until it was the size of a mouse, and the cats played with it, batting it to and fro.

It shrank until it was the size of a small lizard or salamander (or newt or eft). And its protesting voice died away in a faint squeak like the huffle of a snail in danger.

Fredericka stood up and stretched herself and looked down at the shrunken dragon. It was laughable to think of its eating her now. She might more easily have eaten *it*. But she would have disdained to.

It was someone else who did.

As the five children watched in horrified fascination, the smallest kitten pounced on the dragon and gobbled it down as easily as it might have swallowed a fly. Then it looked around with a surprised expression. Then it purred.

"Is that real purr, do you suppose?" said Abbie. "Or is it the dragon growling down there?"

The kitten did not enlighten her. It went hurrying off to join its relations, who were trying to make friends with the field mice in a nearby cornfield (only the mice wouldn't).

And now the crowd, which had been waiting at

a safe distance, came up and surrounded the round gentleman and Mrs. Funkhouser, and more people appeared from the neighboring village, and they all cheered and some let off fireworks.

"Three cheers for the wonderful wizard Oswaldo! And may he reign over us and rule the land forever! Three cheers for the respectable witch, too!" cried all the people.

The round gentleman smiled and bowed and waved his hat. As for Mrs. Funkhouser, she pretended to be fussed and embarrassed, but you could tell she was enjoying the applause just as much as he was.

"That wizard didn't do a thing, really," muttered Abbie to the others, under cover of the noise the people were making. "Mrs. Funkhouser and the cats did it all!"

"I guess that's the way with wizards," said Barnaby. "They let the witches do the work and then take the credit. It's the same way in stories."

"Why, yes," said Fredericka. "Even the Wizard of Oz was a humbug. Remember?"

Then she broke off. She had had an exciting thought. And the more she thought of the thought, the more exciting it was. "You know what?" she said. "This could *be* Oz, back in prehistory times.

Before the books tell about it. Nobody knows *what* it looked like, then. Mr. Oswaldo could even be the real Wizard of Oz. This could be how he got there in the first place. And we're in it from the beginning!"

"But in the book the real Wizard tells Dorothy he came in a balloon," objected Abbie.

"Yes," Fredericka admitted, "but in the book the real Wizard doesn't always tell the truth. Think back."

Everybody thought back.

Fredericka went up to the nearest cheering peasant and tapped him on the shoulder. "Please," she said, "what country *is* this?"

"We be called Dragonland," said the peasant, "up till now, but now all that be changed. Have to think up something new. Oswaldoland, maybe."

"You see?" said Fredericka to the others. "It all works out. The name could have got shortened in the mists of time. Anyway, I'll always think it *was* Oz. I'll feel part of it from now on."

"Or if it isn't," said Abbie, "it's someplace else just as interesting!"

And all agreed.

"And now," said Barnaby, "I guess it's time to go."

"How do we *do* that?" said John.

"I'm not sure," said Barnaby. He went up to Mrs. Funkhouser and the round gentleman, and the other four followed. "Are you really going to stay and rule the country?" he asked.

"I must do as my public demands," said the round gentleman. "They want me. Listen to them cheering."

"I suppose I'll have to stay, too," said Mrs. Funkhouser. "*Somebody*'ll have to see that you're picked up and kept out of trouble!"

"They've offered us a lovely palace," confided the Wizard (if it was truly he). "The one the princesses used to live in that the dragon ate."

"Thirty rooms!" said Mrs. Funkhouser grimly. "Think of the dusting!"

"Come, come, dear lady," said the round gentleman (who might be the Wizard) in rather a lordly way. "The maids of honor will attend to that."

"I," said Mrs. Funkhouser, "have never trusted a maid yet and never will!"

"Could we have our book now?" said Susan. "We'll be taking it home with us. Are you sure you'll be all right here without it?"

"Just let me take one more quick glance," said the round gentleman. He studied the first three or four pages briefly. "There! That'll give me enough new tricks to stay in business for years!"

Susan offered Mrs. Funkhouser a look at the book, but she waved it away.

"I won't be needing it. Just use my common sense. All a matter of good housekeeping."

"What method of travel were you planning to use?" the round gentleman asked the five children.

"That's just it," said Susan. "We're not quite sure."

"Vanishing cream," said Mrs. Funkhouser promptly, without so much as a glance in the book's direction. "There's some in my top bureau drawer." And Fredericka ran to fetch it.

"Shall we let her?" whispered Abbie. "What if we just *vanish*? And don't turn up anywhere?"

"Trust the book," counseled Barnaby. "It's done pretty well so far."

And then Fredericka returned with the jar of vanishing cream, and Mrs. Funkhouser rubbed a little on the foreheads of each.

But Susan clasped the book tight and wished, too, just in case.

You may wonder what vanishing feels like. The answer is that it feels like nothing at all. One second the five children were standing in a magic country (that might or might not be Oz), watching a wizard (who might or might not be *the* Wizard) give a demonstration of One Hundred Easy Card Tricks, while a crowd of peasants cheered.

The next second they found themselves sitting on the front steps of Barnaby and Abbie and Fredericka's little white house in Connecticut.

"Back from the library already?" said Barnaby and Abbie and Fredericka's mother, coming out the door on her way to try to sell someone a split-level colonial ranch house. "You were quick."

"I don't *feel* quick," said Abbie, when her mother had driven off. "I feel as if I'd been away for years. Do you suppose that place really was Oz?"

"If it was," said Fredericka, "I'm disappointed. I'd have thought we'd meet famous people, Dorothy and the Scarecrow and all those."

Barnaby shook his head. "I don't think that's how it works. I think it's more like this. Everybody has to go to Oz—or any other magic country—in his own way. The adventures that are written down in books have already *been*. If we tried to horn in on them, we'd be just tagging along. So we have to make our *own* adventures. It's as if there were different doors."

"That's what the dragon said," said Fredericka dreamily.

"It did?" said Barnaby, interested. "What else did it say?"

"I forget," said Fredericka. "But it was interesting at the time. That dragon had a nice side, in a way. I'm kind of sorry it's gone."

"Maybe it isn't," said John. "Maybe its better self will merge with the kitten."

"Or maybe its *worse* self will," said Abbie. "Maybe the kitten will grow up with man-eating tendencies. They'll have to watch over it and curb it and mold its infant mind."

"Only we'll never know whether they did or not, or what happened." Susan sighed.

There was a silence.

"Anyway, we're started now," said Barnaby. "It's your turn tomorrow."

Susan shook her head. "Tomorrow's Sunday."

"What of it?" said Fredericka. "It's summer. There's no Sunday school."

"Even so," said Susan. "Magic's not a Sunday thing. Not that it's sinful or anything, I don't mean. But they just wouldn't mix."

"How'll we get through a whole day?" said Abbie. "The thought might be father to the wish."

"Better shut the book up somewhere safe," said Barnaby.

"I'm going to," said Susan.

"Without reading the chapter, now it's finished?" Fredericka wanted to know.

"Dwell in the dead past if you want to," Barnaby told her. "I *know* what it says."

"I'd kind of like to look," said John. And he took the book from Susan and began to read.

"It's got illustrations," reported Fredericka, hanging over his shoulder. "Is that what I look like? That isn't what I look like!"

And then the Good Humor man came driving along the road, ringing his bell, and everyone ran to catch up with him, and magic was forgotten in the cooling joy of sheer sherbet.

But first Susan ran across the street to her own house and put the book away carefully in her top bureau drawer.

And later that day, just before supper, without saying anything to the others, she took a walk along lower Weed Street.

As she rounded the familiar bend, she wondered whether she would see a mere hole in the ground where Mrs. Funkhouser's house had been. But to her surprise the house was still there, the same as always. The sign by the driveway was still there, too.

But when Susan came nearer, she saw that the sign didn't say, "Slow. Cats, et cetera" anymore.

The sign said, "For Sale."

And when she went up close to the house and

peered through its windows, she saw that every stick of furniture inside was gone.

It was nice to know that whatever the name of the magic kingdom where Mrs. Funkhouser now reigned, she apparently had her salt and her ammonia and other useful supplies for a respectable witch with her. She had prob'ly moved her possessions to the palace, thought Susan, and then prob'ly she hadn't wanted the house there to remind her of her humble origins; so she had prob'ly rubbed vanishing cream on it, too.

And maybe some of the magic from the book had got *into* the vanishing cream so that it still worked. Or maybe Mrs. Funkhouser (unlike the late dragon) had started believing in her own power so much that she was beginning to be a real witch now, though Susan was sure she would always be a respectable one.

While she was thinking these thoughts, a woman had come out on the porch next door and was regarding her curiously.

"If you're looking for Mrs. Funkhouser and Mr. Oswaldo," said the woman, "they've moved. All of a sudden, as ever was. And they do say," she went on, "that *he*'s gone back into vaudeville."

Susan thought of the round gentleman as she

had last seen him and of Mrs. Funkhouser and her housewifely witchcraft.

"Yes," she said slowly. "Yes, I guess you might say they *both* have. In a way."

And she started walking home.

3

Taming It

"This time no magic kingdoms," said Susan, "and no dragons." And the others (all but Fredericka, who, having survived one dragon, was ready to tackle another) agreed.

It was the second day after the five children had found the book, and they were assembled on John and Susan's front porch.

Sunday had been a day of rest, by Susan's decree.

At first Fredericka had fretted and Abbie had sighed and even Barnaby had wanted to make plans. But Susan had been unusually strong-minded and had put a stop to it.

"If we start all that, we'll be tempted and we might give way," she said. "Let's not even *think* about the magic."

This didn't seem possible, but later it turned out that it was. Books were read and games were played and walks taken, and a few good deeds were even done, to be on the safe side, though nothing good enough or interesting enough to tell about. And the hours passed.

And now at last it was Monday, and here the five children were with the dishes and other chores out of the way and Grannie established at the parlor table just inside the front window with a particularly hard jigsaw puzzle that should keep her out of harm's way for half an hour, at least.

And the time was ripe, and it was Susan's turn.

"No dragons," she repeated, "and no witches. I like it better in the Nesbit stories and those other ones where the magic's more sort of tame."

"Tame is blah," said Fredericka.

"Maybe tame isn't what I mean," said Susan, "but where at first everything starts out real and sort of *daily*. Then when the magic comes it's more . . ." She paused, seeking a word.

"Of a contrast," supplied Barnaby.

There was a silence.

"Aren't you going to ask anything more?" said John.

"I don't want to know any more," said Susan. "I want us just to go about our business and wait for whatever happens."

"There are entirely too many blue pieces in this

puzzle," said Grannie from inside the window. "They can't all be sky or if they are, it's monotonous."

John and Susan went inside and got her started on another corner where some of the blue sky might be somebody's dress. With that settled, the five children left the porch and walked along the road to town as if it were any ordinary Monday.

They passed Mrs. Funkhouser's empty house and discussed where its former occupants were now, and Fredericka wished she had Ozma's magic picture so she might see what they were doing at this moment.

But she did not have the book in her hands; so the picture did not appear.

On Main Street the five children compared finances. Susan had sixteen cents and Abbie had eleven. John had a dollar he'd earned cutting lawns, and Barnaby had fifty cents he'd made selling magazine subscriptions (he had sold one so far). But this money was to be saved toward their college educations.

Still, twenty-seven cents divided by five gave everyone a nickel each with two cents over toward tomorrow. So the candy store was the next stop.

But nothing magic happened there, either (save for the magic that lies in Turkish Taffy and Chocolate Almond-Butterscotch Delight).

It was when they came out of the store and turned the corner that Susan noticed the strangeness first.

"The street's different," she said. "Look."

The others looked.

Instead of short, friendly Cherry Street, with its white houses and big trees, blocks of drab apartment houses stretched far into the distance ahead.

"It's like a city," said John.

"We're somewhere else. It's the magic. It's beginning," said Susan, shivering delightedly. "I like it like this when it sneaks up on you!"

"Where do you suppose we are?" said Fredericka.

"I saw a sign last week that said, 'Watch Our Town Grow,' " said Abbie. "Do you suppose it *did*? Do you suppose this is the *future*?"

A high, gawky-looking windowless car drove past, honking a horn that said "Ah-oo-ga."

John shook his head. "It's the other way round. That's a 1924 Hupmobile," for he was one who knew about such things. "I don't know where we are, but it's in olden times. We're in the past somewhere."

"It's familiar. I've seen this street before. In a book, I think," said Susan. "Only what one?" Then she stopped short and clutched whoever was handy, pointing up ahead.

On the nearest corner stood a little girl. She was

rather a poor-looking little girl, but neat. She wore an old-fashioned apron over her dress, and her dark hair hung straightly down her back in a ponytail. She was looking at something in her hand, something that gave a metallic glint. On the sidewalk nearby sat a fat baby with its thumb in its mouth.

"I *knew* it was a book!" whispered Susan excitedly. "It's the girl in the *Half Magic* picture! It's the little girl in the last chapter who finds the charm after Jane and Mark and Katharine and Martha pass it on!"

"I always wanted to know what happened next!" said Abbie.

"In Oz we got there before the beginning," marveled Fredericka. "This time we're coming in after the end!"

"Shush," said Susan. "Be careful. Don't scare her."

But Fredericka was pushing forward. "Hello," she said. "Do you know what you just found? You just found a magic charm!"

The little girl looked up with a smile. "Hello," she said. "I *thought* it might be that."

"Well, it is," said Fredericka.

"Only it works by halves," said Barnaby.

The little girl shook her head. "It doesn't work at all. I wished I could go into future times and meet some children there, but I'm still right where I started."

"But we *come* from future times!" said Abbie.

"You *do*? Did my wish bring you?" said the little girl.

"I'm not sure," said Barnaby, scratching his head in a puzzled way. The problem of whose wish had brought whom where was too much even for his giant brain.

"You see, we've got a magic of our own," explained Susan, "and we wished at the same time."

"How *interesting*," said the little girl. "Maybe we sort of met in the middle."

"Anyway, we're here," said Fredericka, "and that's the better half of *any* wish."

"Tell me about what it's like," said the little girl. "The future, I mean. Are there no more wars or poor people? Is everything perfect?"

The five children looked at each other.

"Not quite," said Barnaby. "Not just yet. But we're working on it."

"Could I go there and see?" said the little girl. "May I come and call on you?"

"I'm not sure," said Barnaby again.

"Of course we'd be glad to have you, any time," said Susan quickly.

"It's just that in the book Merlin fixed the charm

so it only worked in the present time," said Barnaby.

"Still, that was when the other children had it," said Susan. "Maybe with a new person it'd start all over fresh."

"Who's Merlin?" said the little girl. "What other children?"

"It's a long story," said Barnaby. And he proceeded to tell it to her.

If you have read the book called *Half Magic*, you will know the story Barnaby told. If not, suffice it to say that the charm was an old, ancient talisman that was found lying on the sidewalk by four children in the year 1924 in a town called Toledo, Ohio. And it thwarted them and had its way with them until they learned its ways and tamed it and had *their* way with *it*, traveling through time and space to the court of King Arthur and other interesting places. And in the end six lives were changed. After that the four children left the charm lying on the sidewalk again for someone else to find.

"And you came along and found it," finished Barnaby.

"And we came along and found *you*," said Abbie.

"Oh," said the little girl. She thought for a minute. "How does it work?"

"That's where the catch comes in," said Fredericka.

"It's a wishing charm," said Susan, "only it cuts wishes in two and only grants half of them."

"Like if you wished you were in the middle of London Bridge," said Barnaby, "you might end up just in London somewhere, or you might end up on some other bridge *anywhere*."

"Or the bridge of a ship," said John.

"Or in some dumb old bridge game," said Fredericka.

"Or," finished Barnaby, "you might end up in the middle of the ocean, *halfway* there. So if you want something, you have to wish for twice whatever it is."

"Or twice as much," said Susan.

"Or twice as far," said Abbie.

"Oh," said the little girl again. There was a pause, as all this sank in.

"Do you want any help?" was the eager offer of Fredericka. "Shall I wish for you?"

The little girl looked at her. "No, thank you," she said. "I think I can do it. I've had the two times table." She held the charm before her and addressed it firmly. "I want to go into the future," she said, "twice as far as to the time and place these children come from, and I want them to come there with me. Twice," she added.

"That's very *good*," said Fredericka kindly.

But Susan held their own magic book tight in her hands and wished, too.

The next moment the five children and the little girl were sitting on John and Susan's front porch. I hope it is not necessary to remind you of a seventh person who had been left behind.

"Is this the future?" said the little girl, looking around at white houses, green trees, grass, and a picket fence. "It doesn't seem any different."

"That's cause we're in the country," said Barnaby. "Nature stays pretty much the same. There've been lots of improvements in the world, though. Well, changes anyway."

"Cities are bigger," said Susan.

"Cars go faster," said Abbie. A Thunderbird sped by on the road before them, just to prove it.

"Planes fly higher," said John. "We're exploring outer space now. Of course, you can't see from here," he added, as the little girl looked at the sky expectantly.

"What's that?" said the little girl, pointing upward.

Everyone looked where she pointed, and Susan uttered a cry of alarm.

What "that" was was Grannie, sitting perilously poised on the window sill of John's gable room and washing the window from outside, a thing Susan and John had strictly forbidden her to do.

"Hello," she greeted them. "That puzzle wasn't any good. It wouldn't come out."

"Stay right there," called John, in a voice he hoped was calm. "Don't move."

He ran inside, and Susan and Barnaby and Abbie and Fredericka followed.

If you have never had a grandmother like Grannie (and many have not), you may be wondering about her, and how so active and unexpected an old lady happened to have such calm, sensible grandchildren as Susan and John. In a way, that may be part of the reason. They had learned to remain calm, no matter what.

But if you are thinking of Grannie as just a dotty old lady, you are wrong. She was far more. As to exactly *what* she was, this is not the time or the place to say. That time will come.

For now, it is enough to know that it took five minutes and the combined arguments of all five children to persuade Grannie off the window sill and into the house and downstairs, and establish her in the parlor rocker with some suitable tatting.

"There," said Susan, coming out on the porch again with the others. "Excuse us for leaving you alone." Then she broke off.

The little girl wasn't alone. A man was standing on the front lawn, and the little girl was staring at him in pale surprise.

"Something terrible happened," she cried. "I suddenly remembered I left Baby sitting there on the sidewalk, back home in Toledo, Ohio! So I wished on the charm, but it's all gone wrong. Baby didn't come. *He* came instead!" And she pointed a finger of horror at the man.

"You must have forgotten the half part of the magic," said Susan. "You must have forgotten to say two times everything. You must have brought him *half* here."

"I couldn't have. Does he look like half a baby?"

The five children looked at the man and had to agree that he did not. The man was big, and he wore a suit and a shirt and a tie and a hat. He looked, in short, like a man. But that was at first glance.

As the five children went on looking, the man put his thumb in his mouth. And the little girl gave a cry.

"It *is* Baby! I'd recognize him anywhere! He *always* does that! But what's happened to him?"

"I think I see," said Barnaby. "It could be worse. Just his bottom half might have turned up, or just his top. Or the charm might have brought him all half there and transparent, like the ghost of a baby. It did something like that once before. But it likes to thwart people in a different way each time. So it brought him here half *grown up!*"

"About thirty-seven years old, I'd say," said John.

"Sure! Prob'ly just the age he'd be if he'd really been growing all these years," said Barnaby, "but the half of him that's inside is still just a baby!"

"This is awful!" said the little girl, looking at the babyish man. "I can't take him home again like that! Mother wouldn't *want* him like that!"

"It's very simple," said Fredericka. "All you do is, you make another wish. And get the 'rithmetic part right this time."

"I can't" said the little girl. "When I saw *him*, I was so surprised I dropped the charm, and it rolled down the walk and he picked it up and put it in his pocket. And it's no use asking for it back. Baby'll never give *anything* back!"

She looked at the man, who was now sitting on the grass making a mud pie. Then she burst into tears.

"Don't cry," said John. "We'll get it for you."

"Let *me*," said Susan. After all, it was supposed to be her turn at the magic. And she had always been good with babies.

She went up to the manly form. "Naughty, naughty," she said. "Baby mustn't touch. *Nasty* magic charm. Burney burn. What did Baby do with it? *Tell* Susan."

"How can I?" said the baby (or man). "I can't talk."

Then it looked surprised. "Who said that? Did *I* say that? Why, I can *too* talk!" it said. "Can I walk, too?" It got up and staggered a few steps. "I can walk!" it cried. "Look at me; I'm walking!"

"*Clever* baby!" said Susan. But the man (or baby) paid no heed.

"This is wonderful! I can go anywhere I like!" it boasted. "No more big people carrying me around and telling me what to do! No more everlasting baby carriage! I'm free!" And it started for the gate. Now that it was getting used to walking, it hardly staggered at all.

But the little girl barred the way. "Wait! Stop!" she cried. "Don't you know me?"

The baby looked down at her from its vast height. "Yes, I do," it said. "I know you now. You're that big one that keeps picking me up and carrying me away just when it's getting interesting and putting me to bed. But never again any more of that from now on! From now on I'm bigger than *you* are. I can pick *you* up and carry *you* away!"

And it did.

"Put me down!" cried the little girl, jogging along the road in its overgrown clutch.

"Come back!" called the five children, running to the gate and peering after them.

The man (or baby) was heading down the road in the opposite direction from town, toward the little country railroad station that is called Talmadge Hill.

"Reach in its pocket! Find the charm!" Barnaby shouted after the little girl.

"I can't! He's got me all scrooched!" the little girl called. And after that any further words died away in the distance.

The five children looked at each other.

"Shall we just let them go?" said Susan. "I suppose what happens now is really her adventure, in a way."

"But it's part ours, too," said John. "We helped get them here. Besides, the railway crossing's straight ahead of them. That baby wouldn't know any better than to sit down on the tracks and play dandelion clocks!"

Luckily at this moment the mailman happened along in his truck, and the five children all knew him, so it was all right for them to accept a lift, though aggravating when he stopped at every passing mailbox. At the foot of the hill that led to the station, he turned into a driveway with a special delivery package; so the five children got out and started up the steep hill on foot.

"This is as bad as the dragon," said Fredericka between puffs. "Does somebody have to be kidnapped every time?"

"Who would think a mere baby would be so revengeful?" said Susan.

"It's a 'bad black-hearted baby!' " said Abbie, in the words of the poem by Mr. W. S. Gilbert.

"Maybe it isn't," said Barnaby. "Maybe *all* babies feel like that, if they could express themselves. Maybe they'd *all* turn on us if they could!"

The five children rounded a bend, and the station came into view, with the little girl and the oversize baby in the act of arriving on the platform.

"Oh dear," said Susan. "Suppose a train's just coming in?"

One was.

Seeing the two waiting forms, the engineer brought the train to a stop.

"What if they get on?" said Abbie.

"That baby could disrupt the whole transportation system, if I know it!" remarked Barnaby.

They got on.

Luckily the kind conductor saw the five children struggling up the hill and waited. The children clambered aboard in the wake of their quarry, the whistle went "Toot-toot!" and the little two-car train continued on its way to join the main line.

Traveling with a small child can be difficult at the best of times. When a child looks like a prosperous businessman of thirty-seven but has the heart and mind and soul of a babe of one (if a babe of one could talk), it can be embarrassing to the point of tears. And so the five children now found it.

First the baby chose to sing.

> " 'What does the train say?
> —Jiggle joggle jiggle joggle!
> What does the train say?
> —Jiggle joggle jee!' "

it chanted, in words familiar to all well-read households.

But the words did not awaken a chord in the heart of the lady sitting just behind.

"Really, sir," she said, tapping the baby on its manly shoulder, "if you must bring your children on public conveyances, can't you amuse them in some more quiet manner?"

The shameless infant paid no heed.

> " 'Will the little baby go
>   Riding on the locomo?' "

it chanted.

> " 'Loky moky poky stoky
>   —Smoky choky chee!' "

The lady tapped its shoulder again. "If you are not silent at once," she said, "I shall speak to the conductor!"

The baby turned in its seat and observed the lady. Then it nodded. "I *thought* you'd look like that," it said.

"Why, of all the I never heard!" said the lady.

"I'd complain, Pearl," said her companion.

"I mean to," said the lady.

"Tickets, please," said the conductor, appearing in the aisle.

"Don't want any," said the baby.

"Come, come, sir," reproved the conductor.

"Come *where*?" said the baby, with interest. In a suddenly docile mood it got down from its seat. "Shall we go for a walk now?"

"Certainly not!" said the conductor. "Pull yourself together, sir! *Tickets*, please!"

"Oh, all right," said the baby with a shrug,

taking some already collected tickets from the conductor and putting them in its pocket.

"No, no, no. Give me *your* tickets!" said the conductor.

"Indian giver!" said the baby, handing back the tickets it had taken.

The conductor mopped his brow.

"Conductor," said the lady in the seat behind, "I have been listening to this person's remarks and observing his conduct. In my opinion he is mentally disturbed and no fit guardian for innocent children!"

"You're right, Pearl," said her friend. "In *my* opinion he should be put off the train and his family turned over to the Welfare Society!"

"No, don't do that," said Abbie.

"We'll watch over him better from now on," promised Barnaby. "We'll see that he behaves."

"He's not bad, really," said the little girl. "Just fractious."

"Listen to the poor little things defending him!" said the lady indignantly.

"We'll pay for the tickets, too," said John. "We've got a dollar and a half we earned, between us. Will that be enough?"

"Do you hear that?" cried the lady. "He makes these poor little children work to earn money for him! Oh, how vile!"

"Lowest of the low!" agreed her friend.

"If you ask *me*," said a man in the seat ahead, turning around menacingly, "a father like that is nothing but a skunk!"

"He should be horsewhipped!" said a lady across the aisle, joining in.

"Oh stop! Oh don't! He's *not* our father!" wailed Susan.

"I thought as much!" cried the lady who had been first to complain. "He is probably nothing but a kidnaper! Conductor, arrest that man!"

"Now, now. Keep calm. Order, please," said the conductor. And he turned back to deal with the baby.

But at this moment the baby's eye was caught by something at the farther end of the car, and it pushed past the conductor and ran down the aisle. Barnaby had an alarmed thought and tried to follow, but the conductor was in his way. He hesitated. What would the irresponsible baby do next?

What it did was stop at the water cooler. First it filled a paper cup with water and drank it. Then it started making more cups into paper aeroplanes and sailing them down the car.

"Whee!" said the baby.

"Everybody stay where you are. I'll handle this," said the conductor. And he approached the water cooler.

"Aren't you ashamed?" he said. "Get hold of yourself. Be a man."

The baby seemed to consider this advice. "All right," it said. Then it took the conductor's cap off the conductor and put it on its own head.

The cap seemed to give it a new idea. "I want to drive the train," it announced. "I wish I could drive the train *now*!"

This was what Barnaby had been afraid might happen, all along.

Because, of course, the charm was still in the baby's pocket, but the baby didn't realize its magic power and wouldn't have known the arithmetic to handle it if it had.

What happened next was exactly what you might expect. No sooner did the baby utter its wish than it vanished. In its place appeared the driver of the train, looking around him dazedly.

"What does this mean, Formsby?" said the conductor sternly. "Why aren't you at the throttle? A New York, New Haven, and Hartford man never deserts his post!"

"I didn't," cried the astonished driver. "Did I?" He looked around. "Why, so I did! I don't know how it happened!" Then an expression of horror came over his face. "If I'm here," he said, "then *who is driving the train*?"

The conductor looked at the spot where the baby no longer stood. And he turned pale. "I don't know," he said, "but I have a good idea."

The complaining lady had moved meddlesomely forward, and now she overheard this. "Do you mean to say," she cried, "that we are in the hands of that maniac?"

"We're doomed!" moaned her friend.

And indeed from the actions of the train at that moment, it did truly seem as if they might be.

Of course once the baby wished that it could drive the train, that meant that it could *half* drive it. In other words, it could drive it but not very well. One could only suppose it was trying each of the controls in turn.

The train stalled and started, buckled and bumped, and halted and hopped. Then it got up speed and shot through Cemetery Station without stopping, leaving the waiting people on the platform looking after it with expressions of dismay. Then it reversed and shot past them again backwards, and their faltering faces switched from right to left as if they were watching a tennis match.

By now the hardened commuters, who hadn't noticed anything wrong before, looked up from their papers.

"In all my years of bad service on this railroad,"

said one, "this is the worst yet. I shall write to the Department of the Interior!"

"I," said another, "am saving up money to buy a helicopter."

The conductor was pallid but spunky. "Ladies and gentlemen," he said, "a slight emergency seems to have arisen. But there is no need to panic as yet. Keep your seats and *hang on*!"

And he strode vengefully toward the front of the train.

Barnaby and John and Susan and Abbie and Fredericka and the little girl had all had the same idea, and as the conductor approached the closed-off section where the controls were, he seemed to be knee-deep in children. Several irate passengers had followed the conductor, and there was quite a traffic jam.

"Out of the way," said the conductor kindly but grimly. "It's no use your trying to defend him anymore. This is men's work."

"Don't hurt him," pleaded the little girl.

"If you'd just let us get to him first," urged Barnaby. "You see, he has this charm . . ."

"He has no charm for *me*," said the conductor. "I have seldom met anyone less charming in my life. You had better not watch. This may be painful." And he pushed open the door.

At the controls of the train the utterly emancipated baby pushed at this handle and pulled at that one. It might not be very good at it, but it was enjoying it to the full.

"Jiggle joggle," it sang. "Jiggle joggle jiggle joggle jiggle joggle jiggle joggle . . ."

The conductor and the other men closed in.

Susan and Abbie and even Fredericka admitted afterwards that they did close their eyes during the worst of what followed. But Barnaby and John kept careful watch. So did the little girl.

The conductor and the other men seized the surprised figure at the controls and pinioned its arms. It showed fight, and they strove together.

The scuffle was not a long one. From the pocket of the embattled baby something small and metallic flew forth. Barnaby and the little girl both dove for it and collided. It was John who picked it up, and perhaps this was as well. In her present mood the little girl might have wished herself and the baby twice as far as Toledo, Ohio, and left the others to deal with the maddened train.

But John took things one by one. Considering the circumstances, he did very well.

First he wished the baby were twice itself again. The charm divided the wish neatly in half, and the avenging conductor faltered and fell back as he found himself struggling with a mere one-year-old who squirmed and giggled and crowed in the delight of utter ticklishness.

The conductor rubbed his eyes. So did the irate passengers. And the little girl ran forward and caught the baby up in her arms.

"Oh, Baby, Baby!" she cried. "Forgive me for leaving you behind, and I'll never, never forget you again!"

"Coo," said the baby. And it sucked its thumb.

"Great Scott!" said the conductor. And "What next?" said the passengers.

Next John wished that he and the rest of his party were home again on lower Weed Street. Immediately he and Susan and Barnaby and Abbie and Fredericka and the little girl and the baby found themselves sitting on the porch of the big white house.

"There," said John.

"You're forgetting that poor train," said Susan.

"That's right!" said Fredericka excitedly. "*Nobody's* driving it now. It'll go right to the end of the line and crash!"

"Or even if the driver gets to the controls in time," said Abbie, "think of the effect on the passengers! They're prob'ly all suffering from shock by now. Their poor brains'll prob'ly never be the same!"

"They'll have to go to psychiatrists with traumas," said Barnaby, whose wide reading had taught him many a big word.

So John made another wish, that the train's whole madcap journey would be twice as much as forgotten by all the passengers and crew, and that its morning run would start all over again as if it had never been, only twice as much so. That ought to take care of everything.

And apparently it did, for a second later a "toot-toot" was heard as the train peaceably approached Talmadge Hill station once more.

"The ten twenty-two is late today," remarked Grannie from the parlor window.

"And now may I have my charm back, please?" said the little girl, rather coolly Susan thought.

"What'll we do with it next? Where'll we go?" said Fredericka.

"I think . . ." Susan began, for something, maybe it was the little girl's tone of voice or maybe it was their own magic book, which she still held clutched in her hands, seemed to tell her that the adventure was probably over, at least so far as they were concerned.

But the little girl had begun speaking at the same moment. "I think," she said, "if it's all the same to you, Baby and I'll just go on by ourselves from now on. I think we've had enough of the future."

"I'm sorry things got so wild," said Susan.

"It's not usually that exciting around here," said Abbie.

"It's been an unusual day," said Barnaby.

"All the same," said the little girl, "I think that's what we'll do. Not that it hasn't been interesting," she added politely.

Everyone felt a bit disappointed, but everyone, even Fredericka, could see the little girl's point of view. It was her charm, at least for the moment. Let her use it in her own way while it lasted.

But, "What'll you wish? Where'll you go first?" Fredericka couldn't help asking.

"First?" The little girl's eyes danced as an idea occurred to her. "Well, first I think . . ." She stopped. "Or perhaps . . ." she began again, as another magic possibility flashed through her mind. Then her expression changed. "I think maybe first we'll go home and see Mother," she said. "And after that . . ." She smiled a secret smile at the baby, and the baby smiled back. "After that, we'll see."

She tucked the baby under one arm and held the charm before her in the other hand, poised for flight.

"Do you know the words to say?" asked John.

"Oh, yes," the little girl assured him. "We know everything now, don't we, Baby? We won't make any mistakes from now on." And she wished herself and the baby twice as far as home.

"Good-bye," said Abbie a second later to the spot where the girl and the baby had been standing.

"At least we got them off to a good start," said Susan. "Do you really think she'll be all right? Do you suppose she really won't make any more mistakes?"

"That charm'll find a way," said Barnaby. "It'll foil her somehow, if I know it. But I think," he added, "she'll be all right in the end."

"We never got to explore the past," complained Fredericka. "We never found out that little girl's first name or about her home life or anything."

"It doesn't tell her name in the *Half Magic* book," said Susan, remembering. "So I guess it all works out. I guess we're never meant to know."

There was a silence, as everyone thought about the mysteriousness of things in general and of magic in particular.

"Children," called Grannie from inside the parlor window, "I seem to have tatted myself fast to this rocking chair. Come and unstitch me!"

And the five children ran inside.

4

Losing It

Susan put the book down on the porch before running in after the others. And then, while the five children were untatting Grannie, the front doorbell rang, and it was Eunice Geers, come to show off her new party dress.

Eunice, while not an exciting or a magical girl, was perfectly all right in some ways, and her ways included those of fashion and charm; so after lunch (for which Eunice was pressed to stay), she and Susan spent an enjoyable afternoon in Susan's room, trying on each other's clothes and experimenting with two run-down lipsticks Eunice had rescued from her mother's wastebasket.

Big Pete Schroeder had shown up, meanwhile, with his catcher's mitt and ball, and he and John were tossing a few in the backyard. Barnaby, who was not at his best with a ball, base or any other, sat in the cherry tree and made sarcastic remarks, knowing all the time he should let them alone and go home but somehow not doing it.

Abbie and Fredericka stayed with Grannie and wound yarn while she knitted, meanwhile charming them with tales of life on the old Dakota plains, and how when she was a young girl teaching school, she lived all alone in a sod house, and when she married Grandad, the neighbors moved *his* sod house two miles and joined it on to *her* sod house. Abbie was fond of this story and could never hear it too often.

Later, while Grannie took her nap, Abbie and Fredericka went outside and perched on the front steps, and Hector Hullhorst and Luemma Babcock and little Stevie Wynkoop happened by, and they all played an old-fashioned game called Steps, also known as Red Light (but not to be confused with the other game of that name sometimes referred to in less refined circles as Cheezit).

And unbelievable as it may seem, no one remembered the magic book or thought about it, and many an outsider passed and repassed the fated porch before night fell.

Long before it did, the father of Barnaby and Abbie and Fredericka appeared, home from New York unexpectedly early and with tickets, for both families, to a concert in the neighboring settlement of Silvermine. Barnaby and Abbie and Fredericka were all musical, like their parents, and Susan and John tried to be musical, too, because anything Barnaby liked must be all right. And sometimes when the music wasn't too loud and modern, they found they could follow right along.

Tonight Barnaby's father, who was earning extra money singing in a special television show that week, offered to take everyone to dinner before the concert, at the seafood pier the children all liked, where the big oceangoing yachts and launches docked right alongside. Grannie wore her good black lace with her white hair piled high, and Susan and John were proud of her.

And for the rest of the evening all was lobster and Brahms, and it wasn't till the loud modern second half of the concert that Susan's mind wandered, and she found herself wondering what had become of the magic book and exactly where it was at that moment. She had left it on the front porch when they all ran inside, and she couldn't remember seeing it since. Probably Barnaby had rescued it. After all, it was his turn to wish tomorrow, or Abbie's. But she thought she had better make sure.

What happened next is still a matter of mystery.

Susan claims to this day that she whispered to John to whisper to Barnaby, "You have the book, don't you?" and that Barnaby nodded yes.

John doesn't remember exactly what he whispered. But according to Barnaby the words he heard from John were "You don't have the book, do you?" and he whispered back, "No." If he nodded his head after that, it must have been in time to the music.

What *is* definitely agreed to by everyone is that the fat woman in the row ahead turned around in her seat and said, "Shush!"

And the concert crashed to an end, and everyone went home with Susan sure Barnaby had the book safe, and Barnaby certain it was in Susan's keeping, and both of them wrong.

The next morning Susan woke early with a feeling of joyful expectation. Today would be Barnaby's adventure, or Abbie's. Either way, Barnaby would have an idea. But as the morning wore on, she waited in vain for Barnaby and the others to show up with the book. When ten o'clock came and they still hadn't appeared, she permitted herself the mean thought that it was exactly like Barnaby to hog the whole thing (though this wasn't true, really; Barnaby might boss, but he almost always shared).

"What's the matter?" John finally asked her

frowning countenance as she stalked from room to room. When Susan explained, he shrugged his shoulders.

"What of it? Maybe he's got his reasons. Maybe he can't come over. Maybe he's got chores."

And then big Pete Schroeder stopped by and wanted to go fishing. But first he and John went to dig for worms in the side yard, by the compost heap.

But Susan moped all morning.

Across the street in the little white house, Barnaby was wondering why Susan and John didn't appear with the book. When they didn't, he was about to set out for *their* house, but a shaming thought occurred.

Maybe they were annoyed with him for being surly and making sarcastic remarks yesterday when big Pete Schroeder came by. The fact that he had been in the wrong and knew it made him all the surer that this was probably the trouble. So after battling with his better nature a while, he decided to go and apologize. But when he started down his front steps, he saw John and big Pete come from the other house and wander toward the side yard. So he went indoors again.

"Where *is* everybody? What about the magic?" said Fredericka, happening through the hall.

"There isn't going to be any. Some people would

rather go fishing instead," said Barnaby bitterly. And he went upstairs and into his room and slammed the door.

"The master is cross," Fredericka informed Abbie, which so touched that tender heart that she rapped on Barnaby's door and offered him the rest of her grape No-Cal, which he refused with bare civility.

It wasn't till afternoon that Susan, driven from the house more by sorrow than by anger, was pacing morosely along the road to town when she ran straight into Barnaby, wandering in the opposite direction and kicking a stone ahead of him moodily with the toe of his tennis shoe.

The two eyed each other, at first warily and then with surprise.

"Where's the book?" were the words that sprang to the lips of both.

And it all came out.

Now it was Susan's turn to feel guilty. How could she, always the calm, sensible one, have left their most precious possession on the porch all this time, a prey to the whim of every passing stranger? Needless to say, it was not there now when they ran to look.

Who could have taken it, and what might he have wished?

A conference was called, and both houses were ransacked in vain. John and big Pete Schroeder appeared, without any fish and without the book, either, but this was a surprise to no one. Big Pete Schroeder would be the last to look at a book in any way, shape, or form.

"The thing is," said Barnaby, when big Pete had ambled away homeward, "to make a list of every single person who was on that porch yesterday."

"And then interview them all, like detectives in movies!" cried Fredericka, who could enjoy almost anything so long as it wasn't tame or dull.

Pencils flew, telephone wires hummed, delegations visited this house and that, but the book, as Barnaby put it, remained a thing of the past.

Little Stevie Wynkoop, who was five years old and a very secretive child, caused a false alarm by admitting to having found an old, ancient book and taken it home without permission, but when asked what the book *was*, he declined to say. But Fredericka tracked him to his lair and hounded and harassed him and told him he was adopted (which was untrue) till at last he dug the book out from under a pile of toys and showed it to her. It was a battered copy of *Bunny Brown and His Sister Sue on an Auto Tour* that had come down to Susan from a defunct aunt.

So it seemed the only clue was a fizzle.

"Do you suppose that's all the magic we're going to get?" wondered Abbie. "Did it come into our lives to gladden an hour and then fade like a dream?" (For she had been reading the romantic poets lately, to see how they did it.)

"It can't be," said Fredericka. "It wouldn't be fair. We've hardly had our first magic taste, even."

"Who said magic was fair?" said Barnaby. "It almost never is. But I think it's prob'ly biding its time, just to show us. It'll prob'ly turn up in plain sight some moment when we least expect it."

Susan said nothing. She was too busy feeling remorseful. But Barnaby patted her on the back, which at any other time might have seemed rather insulting but right now was a comfort. And Abbie said, "There, there," and even that helped.

By common consent the five children parted early after dinner and spent a quiet evening. Or at least it started out that way. Susan and John sat in their living room, and Susan hemmed a skirt while John fiddled with a crossword puzzle, which shows how low their spirits had sunk. Grannie sat across from them reading.

Grannie often read in the evenings, tutting to herself when she came to the dangerous parts. Mostly she read anything she could find about the West, not the wild and woolly West of television shows, but the real West she had known as a little girl, seventy or so years before.

Susan had some books by a wonderful woman called Mrs. Wilder, who had lived in a little house in a big woods and later in a little house on the prairie, in the olden times, and when Grannie couldn't find new books about the old West, she frequently read these. They reminded her of herself when she was in her prime, she said.

Perhaps here is as good a place as any to explain about Grannie's character a little more.

It wasn't that she was childish or weak-minded. On the contrary. Her will was almost too strong. It was just that she had been a tomboy for twenty years (even when she was teaching school, which she started at fifteen!) and an active woman for fifty years after that, and now that she was old, she sometimes forgot that she was a tomboy and active no longer.

"I'm still the same, inside," she would explain, when Susan or John begged her to be careful and not climb trees or run or jump.

Susan often thought Grannie must have been a wonderful little girl, and later on an exciting teacher to have, and wished that she could have known her then.

And poetic Abbie once came on a poem that

reminded her of Grannie. It was about a pioneer woman called Lucinda Matlock, who worked hard and played hard and had twelve children and lived to be ninety-six and enjoyed every bit of it. Abbie read it to the others, and they all agreed that it expressed Grannie to a T.

All this made the five children patient when Grannie needed curbing and toning down now.

Tonight as Grannie read, her eyes sparkled and her tutting was louder than usual, causing John to stir restlessly over his puzzle and Susan to look up from her work more than once.

The second time Susan looked up, her glance stayed fixed and her sewing fell from her lap and she must have made a sound, for John looked up, too, and saw what she was seeing.

The book Grannie was reading wasn't one of Mrs. Wilder's stories about Plum Creek or Silver Lake, and it wasn't the new book of Western reminiscences Susan had brought her from the library, either.

It was a red book, smallish but plump, comfortable and shabby and familiar!

So *that* was where the magic book had been all along, thought Susan. Grannie must have found it on the porch and opened it and started to read, and got interested.

But if Barnaby's idea was right and the magic book was different for each person, what was Grannie reading now that made her eyes shine so and brought bright color to her cheeks? A girlhood adventure of her own or of some other pioneer heroine?

Then, just as Susan was trying to stammer out, "What are you reading?" Grannie's gaze left the page, and she stared speculatively before her with the unmistakable expression of an enthralled reader who is about to wish that her book were true and she were part of the thick of it.

John's and Susan's thoughts were as one and their speed was even quicker. Together they sprang across the room just in time to touch the book and add the words "and take us along, too" as the unspoken wish formed itself in Grannie's mind.

And the book did.

There was a whoosh, and the colors of the room ran together and shot up like fireworks. In a second of dazzlement Susan found time to wonder where they'd suddenly find themselves next, in a log cabin in a wolf-haunted woods or on the lone prairie where the coyote howls so mournfully.

The next second she knew the answer.

Where they found themselves was on an open and windy and wintry plain, before a little raw new one-room building that looked exactly like every picture anyone has ever seen of an old-fashioned schoolhouse. John was standing at her side, looking just as startled as she felt.

But where was Grannie?

Apparently nowhere.

In front of the schoolhouse some children were playing Fox and Geese in the hard, crusty snow that carpeted the ground. Leading the game was a tall girl with sparkling black eyes. Next minute the game developed into a snowball fight, and the tall girl pitched snowballs right and left, throwing hard and straight as any boy. Then at the height of the game, when she was victor over everyone else, boys and girls alike, the tall girl stopped throwing, went to the schoolhouse door, and swung a big hand bell. And Susan understood.

Not only was the tall girl the teacher, but the teacher was Grannie, back when she was in her prime!

Susan looked at John, and he seemed to be realizing the same thing. And then the boys and girls started filing into the schoolhouse, and John and Susan filed in after them.

Inside was a potbellied stove by the teacher's desk and two rows of desks and seats, bolted to the floor. The boys sat in one row and the girls in the other, with the littlest down front and the biggest ones in the back (for Grannie, when she was a teacher, had taught all grades at once).

Susan and John found empty seats and sat down.

The first lesson of the day was spelling. Grannie began with the shortest words and the youngest children; so Susan's mind was free to wander. It wandered to Barnaby and Abbie and Fredericka.

It was too bad they would be missing whatever was about to happen. Still, if Barnaby were here, he would have all the ideas and run everything, the way he always did. And apparently the book meant this extra adventure to be just hers and John's and Grannie's.

On the other hand, Barnaby had been awfully good today about Susan's losing the magic book and hadn't made a single sarcastic remark. It didn't seem fair for him and Abbie and Fredericka to be out of it now.

Susan was thinking so hard about this that she forgot to pay attention to the spelling lesson. Suddenly she looked up. The tall girl who was really Grannie was standing at her side, looking down at her, and her black eyes snapped.

"Susan, your thoughts are wool-gathering," she said sternly. "Rise and spell 'xanthophyll.' "

Susan stood up by her desk and blushed. She remembered that in the Little House books "xanthophyll" was the word Laura couldn't spell at the spelling bee, but Pa could. She remembered the whole scene in the book, but she couldn't remember the look of the word.

"I can't," she said. "I'm sorry."

Grannie's young mouth relaxed a little, and her eyes stopped snapping and twinkled. "I couldn't, either, when I was your age," she said, "and it's not a word I've found occasion to use often, since. Still, every piece of knowledge is a piece of knowledge. X-a-n, zan; t-h-o, tho, zantho; p-h-y-double l, xanthophyll. Write it three times on the blackboard and you will remember."

Susan stepped to the blackboard and did as she was told. Grannie moved to the teacher's desk again, and Susan noticed that while she was holding the spelling book in her right hand, her left hand rested on another book, on the corner of the desk. It was a red book, smallish but plump, comfortable and shabby.

As Susan finished writing "xanthophyll" on the blackboard for the third time and turned to go back to her seat, she let her hand brush against the desk (and against the red book) and wished that Barnaby and the little girls would find their way into this adventure somehow.

Later on she was to be glad that she had. Right now she turned her mind to the next lesson.

The next lesson was arithmetic, and John was standing by his desk struggling to divide 264 by 12 when the door opened and three figures walked in. The three figures looked startled, to say the least, and as if they weren't sure how or why they had come.

"Good morning," said Grannie from the teacher's desk. "You are new pupils?"

"I guess so," said the largest figure.

"This is not a guessing game," said Grannie sternly. "Say 'Yes, ma'am.' What is your name?"

"Barnaby," said the figure, "and she's Abbie and she's Fredericka."

"Barnaby, Abigail, and Fredericka," said Grannie, "you may find seats. I shall not mark you tardy since it is your first day, but be on time in future."

Fredericka found the last empty seat, down front. Susan moved over quickly and patted the place beside her, and Abbie, with a look of grateful recognition, slid into it. John was still standing by his desk to recite and was so startled at seeing Barnaby that he made no move. But a boy called Clarence Oleson moved over and patted the place by *him*, and Barnaby took it. Susan's heart misgave her. She did not trust Clarence Oleson's expression.

"We will resume the recitation," said Grannie.

As John went on with his problem, Abbie whispered, "Where are we? What's happening?"

"It's the magic," Susan whispered back. "Grannie found the book and wished. She's the teacher, back when she was in her prime."

"Silence," said Grannie, in no uncertain tone.

After that, silence reigned until recess.

During recess, John and Susan and Barnaby and Abbie and Fredericka met in conference, and John and Susan told the others everything that had happened. And then Clarence Oleson came swaggering up and proved to be just as mean as Susan had thought he would be from his look.

"Well, you're a little sawed-off hunk of nothing, aren't you?" he said to Barnaby. "Are you called Barnaby because you were born in a barn? On *our* farm we always drown the runt of the litter!"

Barnaby's hands made fists, and he moved toward Clarence. But John got between them.

"Lay off," he said.

"I can take care of myself," Barnaby muttered angrily.

"I know you can," said John. "But right now you're not going to."

"Who asked *you*?" said Clarence. "No big galoot

of a new boy is going to tell *me* what to do." And he reached past John to tweak Barnaby's ear.

At that moment Grannie appeared in the schoolhouse door. Her eagle eye rested coldly on Clarence for a moment, but she said nary a word and merely rang her hand bell. Recess was over, and the children trooped back inside.

After recess, Clarence's behavior continued at a low level. The lesson was reading preparation, and Clarence kept pushing sideways in his seat, crowding Barnaby over till he was right at the edge. Then Clarence made a sudden movement, and Barnaby sprawled crashingly into the aisle.

Grannie looked up sharply at the sudden noise. Clarence was sitting far over on his own side by now, with an innocent expression on his face.

"Silence," said Grannie.

Barnaby picked himself up and his hands made fists again, but he kept his control and started to study once more.

Next Clarence produced a pin and stuck Barnaby with it hard.

This was the last straw, and Barnaby hit him.

I have said that Barnaby was not at his best with his fists. But in this case righteous anger lent strength to the blow. And Clarence hadn't expected a sawed-off little runt to show fight and was taken by surprise.

"Teacher," he bawled, only partly in pretense, "he hit me!"

"Barnaby," said Grannie. "Come here."

Barnaby went there.

"Hold out your hand."

Barnaby held it out. Grannie produced a ruler and hit his hand three times, quite hard.

"There is to be no fighting in class," she said sternly. "Remember that."

Barnaby's face was white, but he kept his voice steady. "Yes, Teacher," he said. He couldn't very well say, "Yes, Grannie," and he had forgotten Grannie's maiden name, if he ever knew it.

Grannie regarded him, and her grim expression softened. She smiled slightly and nodded to herself as if in approval. "Good," she said. "And now . . ." and she produced an extremely large pin from her desk, "you may take this and stick Clarence with it."

There was a murmur of awe from the whole class.

Barnaby looked at the pin. Then he looked at Clarence with distaste. "I couldn't," he said.

"Very well," said Grannie. "Then *I* shall!" And she advanced down the aisle, pin in hand. With her black eyes snapping and her splendid tall handsomeness, she presented a truly terrifying picture of justice aroused and on the warpath, and Clarence fairly writhed in anticipation.

"Please, Teacher, don't!" he cried. "I'm sorry, honest, Teacher!"

Grannie (or Teacher) eyed him with contempt. "So you can't take your own medicine, eh?" she said. "In that case, hold out your hand." And she hit his hand *four* times with the ruler, harder than she had hit Barnaby's.

The murmur of awe and admiration in the room swelled to what was almost a cheer.

"Silence!" said Grannie. "Barnaby, you may sit with John in future."

Barnaby slid into half of John's seat, and the class quieted down. But Abbie could not contain her feelings. "She *is* like Lucinda Matlock," she cried in Susan's ear, "in the poem! She's just a wonderful strong pioneer woman of America! I always said so!" Then she broke off as she felt Grannie's gaze upon her.

"Abigail," said Grannie, "you have something to tell the class?"

Abbie hung her head and blushed. "I was saying," she stammered, "that you remind me of a poem."

"Indeed?" said Grannie. "Then pray recite it for us. You may rise."

Abbie stood up. "Well, I'm not sure I'll remember all of it," she said, "but I'll try." And she did.

If you would like to know the whole poem that Abbie recited, you may find it in a book called *Spoon River Anthology*. But it had not yet been written when Grannie was in her prime, and she listened to Abbie's recitation with interest, particularly to the last part where it says:

"What is this I hear of sorrow and weariness,
Anger, discontent and drooping hopes?
Degenerate sons and daughters,
Life is too strong for you—
It takes life to love Life."

"Humph!" said Grannie, when Abbie had finished. "Not much of a poem, if you ask me. It doesn't even rhyme."

"Nowadays poets *don't*, always," said Abbie bravely.

"Lazy things!" sniffed Grannie. "Mr. Longfellow would never do such a thing. Or Alfred Lord Tennyson. Still, what it says is perfectly true. It *does* take life to love life. Remember that, all of you."

The class nodded as if hypnotized. As for Abbie, looking at that splendid young face and those blazing eyes and thinking of the long, full life Grannie was still to have, she was sure that one person, at least, would always remember.

Everyone's attention had been so riveted on Grannie and Abbie and the poem that almost no one had noticed a sound that was beginning to be heard outside. But John, always one for noticing things, had noticed. The sound was the sound of wind rising.

His eyes went to the window, and he half got up from his seat, raising his hand.

"Please, ma'am," he said. "There's a storm coming up."

Now as the others looked, the window went blank with the snow that was darkening and thickening the air. The sound of the wind rose to a howl. And Susan knew, from reading about them in the Little House books, that one of the terrible sudden prairie blizzards had come.

"Children," said Grannie with quick decision, "I am going to dismiss school while there is time to get back to town. Go and get your coats."

Everyone ran to put on coats while Grannie dealt with the dampers of the coal stove. When Grannie opened the door, the wind took Susan's breath away. No one could see a foot before his face, but Grannie turned toward town and started forward.

"All join hands and follow me," she said, taking Susan's hand in hers.

Abbie found herself next to Barnaby in the line. "Take my sleeve," he told her. He seemed to be holding something in his hand, but Abbie couldn't see what it was through the blinding, muffling snow.

The children staggered on into whirling blackness for what seemed like hours and was probably all too many minutes.

"I'm afraid we've lost the way," Grannie finally shouted. The wind carried her voice away, but Susan could just make out the words.

Behind them Barnaby seemed to be trying to free his sleeve from Abbie's grasp in order to do something or other with whatever it was he held in his hand, but Abbie hung on tight and he couldn't.

Suddenly Susan tripped and fell forward into comparative dryness. "In here!" she called.

The others followed her into the opening she had stumbled upon. Grannie had thoughtfully brought matches and a tinderbox with her, and now she struck a light. For a moment Susan couldn't imagine where they were. Then she realized. She and the others were inside a sod house built into a bank, like the one Laura lived in in *On the Banks of Plum Creek*. Susan recognized it from the picture in the book.

"It must be a deserted claim house," said Grannie. "We must have turned the wrong way. Now we're farther from town than ever."

"At least we're dry," said Fredericka.

"And warm," said Abbie, for inside the sod house it was surprisingly cozy.

"Maybe whoever held the claim left a lamp," said John.

He and some of the other boys searched and found one lamp with a little oil in it. Grannie lit the lamp and counted noses. All the children of the class were here and safe.

"But these storms last three or four days sometimes, don't they?" said Barnaby. "Did the person who left the lamp leave any food?"

Everyone searched again, but no food was to be found. For the moment they were dry and comparatively warm, but if the storm went on, how long could they last?

"Well," said Barnaby slowly, "I had an idea. I thought we might get lost, and I brought this." And he showed what he had been holding in his hand.

What he was holding was the hand bell from the schoolhouse.

The young teacher who was really Grannie looked from the bell to Barnaby with a peculiar expression, rather as if she didn't know whether to be angry or glad.

"Taking school property without permission is

against the rules and you must be punished," she said finally, in a voice that was just as peculiar as her expression. "Hold out your hand."

Barnaby held out his hand.

The teacher who was Grannie looked around rather distractedly as if she expected to find her ruler somewhere in the air. Then she slapped Barnaby's palm once with her own strong hand. Then she looked sorry.

"All the same," she said, "it was a very good idea, and I should have thought of it myself." And she shook the hand she had struck warmly.

"And now," she went on, turning to the others, "everyone stay safe inside here while I ring the alarm from the doorway."

"Can't I ring?" said Barnaby. "I thought of it."

"We could take turns," said John.

And in the end that is what they did. But Grannie, as teacher in charge, made a rule that the person ringing the alarm mustn't wander out of sight of the doorway and mustn't stay outside for more than five minutes at a time by her watch, for fear of freezing.

When it was Susan's turn to ring the hand bell, she gasped as the wind of the blizzard struck her. She had forgotten for a moment how cold and loud it was. Surely no one would hear her ringing through all this howling. But she swung the hand bell as hard as she could. Then she listened. Was that a sound, far away, beyond the wind's uproar? She rang again and listened once more. The sound, if it was a sound, seemed nearer.

"It's my turn again now," said Barnaby, surprising her by appearing at her side and shouting in her ear.

"Listen," shouted Susan. She let Barnaby swing the hand bell this time. Then they both listened.

"Sleigh bells!" cried Barnaby. "Someone's coming! Better get inside in the warm and tell the others!"

And "Sleigh bells!" Susan cried, running into the sod house. Now Grannie and the others crowded round the door, and everyone took turns ringing as loud and strong as each one could. Always when the hand bell stopped, the sleigh bells seemed closer.

At last a sleigh loomed big and darker than the snow around it, and someone called, "Quick! Hop in!"

"Why, forevermore!" cried Grannie. "Carl Ingoldsby! What are you up to, catching your death of cold gallivanting around in this weather?"

Susan looked at John and John looked at Susan.

Carl Ingoldsby had been the name of Grannie's husband, the grandfather Susan and John had never seen, who had died and been buried out on the Western plains long ago. And yet here he was, young and come a-courting, or at least a-rescuing!

"Save your breath and get in!" shouted Carl Ingoldsby, just as snappily as Grannie had shouted at him.

And somehow Grannie and all the children crowded into the sleigh.

Carl Ingoldsby turned the horses, and they went trotting off into the whirling blackness. Apparently Carl Ingoldsby knew the way, even in a blinding snowstorm. Or perhaps the horses had a sense that would guide them home.

Whichever was true, before long the lights of the little town on the prairie showed faintly ahead. Carl Ingoldsby seemed to know where each child in the school lived, and the sleigh stopped at house after house until only John and Susan and Barnaby and Abbie and Fredericka were left. And of course Grannie.

Susan was just wondering what would happen to *them* and whether they would be set down on a cold dark Main Street, to find their way home through the years to the future, when the horses dashed into the open doorway of a stable. She could see it was a stable because a lantern hung by the door, but once inside, darkness reigned again and Susan could hardly make out the forms of Grannie and Carl In-goldsby, where they sat looking at each other. Nei-ther one made a move to get out of the sleigh.

"Thanks for the sleigh ride," said Grannie, rather airily Susan thought.

"Don't mention it," said Carl Ingoldsby. "Happy to oblige. Anytime."

There was a silence.

"I suppose . . ." Grannie's voice broke off and hesitated. "I suppose you saved all our lives, in a way."

"Oh, I don't know," said Carl Ingoldsby. "The storm might have stopped. Or somebody else might have found you."

"Well, thanks anyway," said Grannie.

There was another silence.

"What," said Carl Ingoldsby, "if I were to ask you to ride home again someday?"

"Why not try asking," said Grannie, "and see?"

Carl Ingoldsby gave a chuckle. "Independent, aren't you?" he said.

"Yes," said Grannie. "I am."

"What," said Carl Ingoldsby, "if I were to ask you to ride home with me someday and *stay*?"

This time the silence lasted a long while. Susan's eyes were accustomed to the darkness of the stable now, and she could see that Carl Ingoldsby's arms were around the young Grannie, and she was not resisting. And Susan noticed something else.

All through the school day and all through the storm and the sleigh ride Grannie had held the magic book clutched in one hand. Now the book fell from her grasp as she put her hand up to touch Carl Ingoldsby's cheek.

And Susan picked it up.

As she said afterwards, anybody could tell the adventure was over.

And of course once the book was in Susan's hands, it left off being the true Western story it had been for Grannie and became the old familiar magic book the five children had come to know and distrust so well. And Susan wished.

This time there were no colors to run together and shoot up like fireworks. The dark stable merely became darker. And then it was as if someone had switched the light on again.

There were Susan and John, at home in their living room, and there was Grannie, rocking and dozing in the chair across from them.

As Susan watched, Grannie woke with a start. Then a smile spread slowly over her face. "I must have been dreaming," she said.

Susan and John felt very much the same. And yet if it had been a dream, how had the book come from Grannie's hands to Susan's, where it now sat safe and fat and red and mysterious?

Grannie was still smiling. "I was dreaming of your grandpa," she said. "He was a fine-looking man. Fine pair of hands with a team of horses, too. Fine man, generally." Then she struggled up from her chair. "Time for bed," she announced. "Where's that book I was reading?"

Susan held the magic book concealed and went to fetch the book of Western reminiscences from the library. "You mean this one?"

Grannie took the book. "It'll do. It's not the one but it'll do." And she suffered herself to be helped upstairs.

Later on John caught Susan alone for a moment in the upstairs hall. "Do you suppose Barnaby and the others got back, too?" he wondered. "Do you suppose they think it was a dream, too? Or would they know?"

It was too late to call, for Barnaby's father always went to bed early when he had a big television show next day, and the bell would wake him.

But at that moment John and Susan's telephone rang. Susan got there first.

"Oh good, you're back, too," said Barnaby's voice. "So are we."

"That was nice, wasn't it?" said Susan.

"Yes it was," said Barnaby.

There was a remembering pause.

"We'll be over early tomorrow with the book," Susan told him. "Is it your turn next or Abbie's?"

There was another pause, this time as of inner struggle. Then Barnaby's better nature asserted itself. "Ladies first," he said. "I'll go tell her." And he hung up.

Susan reported this conversation to John, and then stopped in for a good-night look at Grannie.

Grannie was already asleep. Apparently she was really dreaming now, for there was a smile on her face. And as Susan watched, she murmured in her sleep.

"Mrs. Carl Ingoldsby," she said.

Susan smiled, too, and switched off the lamp.

5

Thwarting It

When Barnaby came into Abbie's room, she was already in bed (for he had tiptoed downstairs to the telephone in his stocking feet, after all the lights were out and their parents were asleep).

But once he'd whispered the news that it was her turn next, she stayed awake thinking for a long time. The adventure with Grannie had been the best yet, maybe because part of it had been serious as well as fun. Where could she wish them tomorrow that would be even better?

So far the book's magic had been sort of bookish, the adventure that was more or less Oz and the *Half Magic* one, and then the Little House books mixed up with Grannie's own life. Maybe that was the book's secret. Maybe it made only book magic because it was a book itself.

Abbie went over her favorite reading in her mind. There were the Betsy-Tacy series and *When Molly*

Was Six (which had been her mother's own favorite when *she* was a girl). But somehow Abbie felt that Barnaby and John and Susan and even Fredericka would not appreciate a visit with the classic heroines of these.

Poetry usually held the answer to most things.

"*Hiawatha?*" No, Abbie had had enough of primitive America for a while. "*Evangeline*" was too sad. "*The Lady of the Lake*" had a good story and "*The Eve of Saint Agnes*" was thrilling (though full of hard words) but neither wildest Scotland nor romantic Italy seemed quite perfect for a day's outing. And thinking dreamily of Roderigh Vich Alpine and jellies soother than the creamy curd, Abbie fell asleep.

Wondering a lot about tomorrow the last thing at night often makes a person wake early and eager to begin it. You might try this plan the night before your next arithmetic exam. Of course, sometimes it works the other way and you toss on a sleepless pillow only to turn slothful with the dawn. This is not advised, before an exam or at any other time.

But for Abbie on Wednesday morning the former was the case, and she was up and around and down by half-past six with her bed made and her own breakfast eaten. So that when her mother came downstairs ten minutes later to get breakfast for her father, coffee and eggs were already bubbling on the stove, and the toast was in the toaster and the honey in the pot.

Her mother thanked her and said she could come along on the ride to the station, a thing Abbie always liked to do, for her father was a very special person to her, and indeed to all the family.

This morning, when he came into the kitchen all dressed up in his city clothes, Abbie thought again how handsome he was and how nice, and with that beautiful voice, and wished, not for the first time, that the important television people would discover this about him, too. (But she did not have the book in her hands at the moment, as it was still at Susan's house; so the wish did not count as a magic one.)

If the important television people discovered how wonderful her father was, maybe they would let him sing solos all by himself and he would make more money and her mother wouldn't have to work so hard selling houses and could stay home, and maybe her father could be home more, too.

Of course if he were a solo singer, he would still have to work hard, but maybe it would be at more reasonable hours, and he wouldn't always be running for the seven-twelve and not getting home till the eight thirty-four, just in time to kiss Abbie good night.

And there was more to it. Her father seemed happy in his work and was almost always cheerful and fun, but Abbie knew that standing in the background and singing in the chorus, or a quartet, wasn't really what he had studied for all those years and hoped to be.

The reason she knew this was that she and her father had a secret.

"*Why* won't they let you sing by yourself, ever?" Abbie had said once, when they were alone. "You're just as good as any of them."

"Well," her father had said, "I don't know about that. But in the first place, I'm too short." To be a leading man, he told her, a person had to be tall, or at least above middle height. Unless he were a comedian, and Abbie's father, while often funny around the house, was not that.

"But don't say anything about it to the others," he went on. "Let's have it be a secret between you and me."

The reason for not telling the others was that Barnaby was too short, too, and his father didn't want him to worry about it. Probably he would choose a career where it didn't matter.

"What about *me*?" Abbie said. "I'm short, too. So's Fredericka."

But her father told her that for a girl being too

short wasn't a bad thing and was even at times considered to be a good one. It didn't seem fair.

This morning, as they stood on the station platform (for the seven-twelve was late for once and her father didn't have to run), Abbie thought to herself that he didn't look too short to *her*. And she made one more try.

"Daddy, you know where the microphone is. Why don't you just walk straight down to it and *sing*? Then they'd *know*!" she said.

"All right, I'll remember that. Maybe I will," said her father. But Abbie could tell from the loving note in his voice and the way she felt him exchanging a smile with her mother above her head that he was only humoring her. And then the seven-twelve screamed twice and came into the station, and her father kissed her and her mother good-bye and went gallantly off, holding himself straight and looking as tall as he could, as if he were in front of the television cameras already.

But Abbie went on thinking about him all the way back to the little white house.

Barnaby and Fredericka were up by this time and busy with their own breakfast and chores, and Abbie helped them, but her mind wasn't on her work and she served Barnaby Rice Krispies, which he wholly detested, instead of Bran Flakes, and let

Fredericka make her bed without any hospital corners at *all*.

And then their mother went off to her office and Susan and John arrived, and Susan handed over the book, and for the next half hour all was squabble and shove as four eager voices surrounded Abbie, advising her what to wish and how to wish it. Abbie's mildness had that effect on people.

But this morning was different.

"Let's go see the Three Musketeers," John suggested, and "Through the mountain with Bilbo Baggins the Hobbit," shouted Fredericka. Apparently everyone else had come to the same conclusion Abbie had, that the book preferred to take its lucky masters down the ways of *other* books.

"*At the Back of the North Wind*," said Susan, tempting Abbie very much, for she had often longed to go adventuring with the North Wind and Diamond, as has every reader of the great book of that name (except for the ending part, which is sad).

But she shook her head stubbornly to each and every offer.

"All right, where *do* you want to go, then?" said Barnaby finally.

"To New York," Abbie told him, "and watch Daddy's television show."

"Oh, for heaven's sake!" said Barnaby in disgust. "If *that's* all you want, why didn't you just go in with him on the train?"

"He wouldn't have taken me," said Abbie sadly. "He never will."

And this was true. Their father always said that it was bad enough looking at the programs on the set at home, but as for watching rehearsals, some depths were better left unplumbed, and he would protect them from the seamier side of life as long as he could. Which was a joke, and yet at the same time Abbie and Barnaby and Fredericka knew that he wasn't really joking.

"He wouldn't want us to do it," said Barnaby now. "Besides, we can't. It wouldn't be a magic thing."

"I think television *is* magic," said Abbie, "or how do you explain it?"

Barnaby couldn't. His ideas were literary rather than scientific. "But the book only makes book magic," he objected.

"How do you know?" said Abbie. "We haven't *tried* anything else."

"I heard somebody say," put in Fredericka, "that someday pretty soon there won't *be* any books. Television'll take their place."

Everybody shuddered at this thought.

"It won't," said Barnaby. "It couldn't. And I

don't think we ought to do anything to encourage it and make it think it can."

"I know," said Abbie. "I don't think we should, either. But that's still the wish I want. I want to see the rehearsal, and then I want to see the show."

She had another wish in mind, too, for later on, but she said nothing about it now. Wait till the time.

John and Susan and Fredericka were looking at her with a new respect and as if they hardly recognized her. Abbie had never been so stubborn before or struck out on such an original tack, either. And even Barnaby seemed to be weakening.

"Well," he said, and broke off, hesitating. He turned to John and Susan. "What do *you* think?"

"I worry about leaving Grannie," said Susan. "Won't all that take the rest of today and tonight, too?"

"That doesn't usually matter, with magic," John pointed out. "When we get back, it's usually still the same time it was when we left."

"It might not be *this* time," said Barnaby. "If you ask me, making book magic stoop to television would be thwarting it in the worst way. It might turn on us. Still . . ." And he broke off, hesitating again. Abbie could see that he would like to watch Daddy in the show, too.

"Let's see what Grannie's doing now," said Susan, and all five children ran across the street to the big house.

In the living room Grannie was reading her Western book and hardly looked up when the five children trooped in. This was encouraging, and yet there was no knowing what ideas the book might put into her head to go and do, next minute. Of course, after seeing Grannie in her prime last night, the children felt a new respect. There didn't seem to be much that she couldn't do and do well. But she might forget that she was in her prime no longer. Susan was in a quandary.

But at that minute there was a rap at the door, and it was Grannie's friend Miss Centennial Peterson from down the road, wanting Grannie to come to lunch with her and stay for supper. Miss Centennial was lots younger than Grannie, only seventy-one and still in her first vigor. So *that* was all right.

"You see, it all works out," said Abbie, when Grannie's knitting and her other goods and chattels had finally been collected and she had been speeded on her way. "We're *meant* to go."

"All right," said Barnaby. "It's on your own head."

"But let's have lunch first," said Fredericka, for they had been arguing so long that by now it was way past noon.

A sort of picnic meal was rounded up in the kitchen, and everyone hurriedly chipped in to do the dishes (and chipped three plates in the process).

And at last Abbie stood with the book in both hands, and everyone watched respectfully while she made her wish.

The next moment the five children were in the middle of the television show, in the middle of rehearsal.

Abbie's father always said that once you saw what went on behind the scenes at a television show, it was a wonder to you that anything ever came out on the air at all.

And looking around now at the confusion on every hand, the children could only agree.

In one corner dancers danced. In another singers sang (and Abbie and Barnaby and Fredericka's father was one of them). On the stage jugglers juggled and acrobats sprang. Several stars of stage and screen sat here and there, looking important and waiting their turn.

And around and among and between these wandered the director, talking every minute and giving orders, with his secretary at his elbow taking down every golden word.

Abbie had wondered if their presence would

pass unnoticed and whether she should have included something about this as part of her wish. But luckily there were some child actors waiting to rehearse in one of the sketches, and she and Barnaby and John and Susan and Fredericka sat with these and tried to look like child actors, too.

Fredericka attempted to make friends with the child actors, but they were too busy combing their hair and complaining about their costumes and listening to their mothers' advice about how to steal the audience's attention from the other child actors and made little reply.

And then Abbie said "Shush" as her father appeared on the stage with some of the other singers. And even Fredericka quieted down.

The number that was being rehearsed was a song by a famous rock 'n' roll star. While the star squirmed and writhed and sang (if you could call it that), four men singers swayed back and forth behind him and hummed or uttered nonsense syllables to a counter melody. This is what is known in musical circles as a vocal background.

Looking at the stage, Abbie had to admit that her father was the shortest man on it. But he looked the nicest, too.

And then, because one of the chords sounded

wrong, the director had each of the quartet sing his part alone, while the rock 'n' roll star fidgeted and bit his nails and looked bored.

The words of the vocal background were not edifying.

"Chickadee tidbit, chickadee tidbit,
  Skedaddle skedaddle pow!"

the men warbled in turn, on different notes and in different voices.

But when Abbie's father's turn came, his voice rolled out so deep and rich and true that her heart ached with love, and she was sure the important people would discover how wonderful he was right then and there, without any help from the magic at all.

This did not happen. All the director said was, "O.K. Take it straight on from there."

So Abbie held the book tight and wished the important part of her wish. What she wished was that the important people would discover her father tonight before the show was over.

"I'll let you know when," she told the book.

At that moment the director's assistant appeared at the children's elbow. "All right, kids, get up there," he said. "It's time for your bit now." And the child actors trooped obediently stageward.

"You, too," he added, as Abbie and the others remained in their seats. The five children looked at each other, shrugged, and followed the crowd.

Exactly what the act was that they were supposed to be a part of, Abbie and Barnaby and Fredericka and Susan and John never knew. Apparently the child actors were expected to crowd around the rock 'n' roll star and ask for his autograph. But Abbie and Barnaby and Fredericka and Susan and John had no interest in his autograph, or him either, and they didn't know what lines to say or where to stand, and they were afraid any minute Abbie's father, who was still on stage, would recognize them.

So they stayed as far away from the rock 'n' roll star as they could and huddled together and hid behind each other and bumped into the other child actors and got in their way until the scene was one of utter confusion, and the director pushed around what hair he had in a frenzy.

"What do you kids think you're doing up there?" he shouted. "No, I mean you. *You* five." Then he started counting. "I didn't order that many kids. Those five must be gate-crashers. How did they get in here?"

Everyone in the studio now turned to look at the five children, and everyone included Abbie and Barnaby and Fredericka's father. He looked, looked again incredulously, and started forward. Abbie clutched the book to her and begged it to help. And it did, in the simplest way it knew.

Abbie's father stopped short, blinking. And the director said, "Where are they? Oh, they've gone. Good riddance."

"What's up?" hissed Fredericka.

"We're invisible, I *think*," said Abbie. "To *them*, I mean." (For they could still see each other perfectly well.)

"And now," said the director, "where was I?" Then he sank into a chair. "It doesn't matter. I can't go on. Those kids have shattered my mood. Might as well break for dinner now. Everybody be back in one hour."

And the crowd started filing out the doors.

Fredericka now suggested that there were all manner of interesting things five invisible children could find to do in a deserted television studio. "We could broadcast from coast to coast. I'll do my scarf dance."

But Barnaby told her sternly that they'd caused enough trouble already, and they'd better make themselves scarce from now on till the actual program began.

So the five children left the studio and wandered out into the street, which happened to be Broadway.

New York City has a magic of its own, even when you are not a child and not invisible. When you *are*, it is even better. And John and Susan and Barnaby and Abbie and Fredericka now tasted it to the full.

They pressed unseen through the madding crowd, causing people to cry, "Who're you pushing?" to other people who hadn't been pushing one bit. They rode the subway to Forty-second Street, changed trains, and rode back again. They walked a block across town and gazed upon the topless towers of Rockefeller Center. They entered a doughnut shop and invisibly ate doughnuts and paid for them with invisible hands until quite an interesting panic spread among the city's other doughnut-fanciers.

During the stroll, Abbie was with them in body but not in spirit. She was too busy watching all the clocks they passed and waiting for it to be time to get back to the studio.

Eventually it was, and the five invisible forms entered the theater part and secured seats in the front row. When people came and sat on their invisible laps they squirmed and made their invisible knees as knobbly as possible till the people moved away, saying, "Wouldn't you think the television company could afford *springs*? I'm going to write to Mr. Minow!"

And at last the drums rolled and the spotlights beamed and the grand super-spectacular transcontinental variety show began.

During the early moments Abbie's father was not conspicuous. In the opening number he stood in the back row. In the next two songs he was part of a group that sang vocal backgrounds out of range of the camera. Halfway through the program he carried on a tree that was part of the scenery. He did this so well and so neatly that Abbie wanted to applaud, but she restrained herself. The time would come.

And it did, with the entrance of the rock 'n' roll star, whose number was to be the finale of the show. He began his song, and Abbie's father and the three other men danced onto the stage behind him. Abbie waited till her father was right next to the star, so his face would surely show in the camera. Then she looked at the book.

"Now," she told it.

The next moment, on the great stage and in the living rooms of fifty million television fans throughout the country, a surprising scene took place.

The rock 'n' roll star squirmed and writhed, as was his habit, but no sound fell from his lips. The four singers swayed behind him and their mouths made words, but no sound came from three of *them*, either.

Only Abbie's father's voice rang out over the nation, sounding richer and truer than ever.

> "Chickadee tidbit, chickadee tidbit,
> Skedaddle skedaddle pow!"

he sang. And again,

> "Chickadee tidbit, chickadee tidbit,
> Skedaddle skedaddle pow!"

A look of surprise appeared on his face as he realized something unusual was happening, but he went right on, just as he had been rehearsed to do.

> "Chickadee tidbit, chickadee tidbit . . ."

Abbie's heart nearly burst with pride in him and in herself, too. He was her father and he was singing a solo on television at last, and now the whole world would know how wonderful he was, and she had done it!

"Good girl!" breathed Barnaby in her ear, as he realized what her wish had been. Fredericka got the idea only a second later and clutched Abbie's arm. Susan and John, not being musical, needed to be explained to.

As for the studio audience, first it gave a gasp of surprise. Then a wave of delighted laughter swept through it, followed by a burst of applause that grew and grew and kept right on till the end of the program. When the child actors pranced on for their little closing bit, not one word they said could be heard.

And even when the show was over, the audience didn't seem to want to stop clapping.

"That little fellow sang right out!" said the man behind Abbie. "He took his part good!"

"He was better than the star, if you ask me," said the woman next to him.

As for Abbie, she could hold herself back no longer. She left her seat and ran right up the steps onto the stage, and the other four were not far behind her.

Her father stood in the center of the stage, surrounded by the director and the star and what looked like a hundred other people, all talking at once and waving their arms and undoubtedly congratulating him on his success.

And as Abbie looked at his nice puzzled, modest face, she forgot to be proud of what she'd done and just thought what a wonderful father she had, and not too short at all.

And she ran straight toward him.

6

Being Thwarted

Abbie ran straight toward her father. Then she stopped.

The director and the star and all the other people weren't congratulating him. They were angry.

"You sang in the wrong place!" the director was shouting. "You spoiled the whole show!"

"I didn't," said Abbie's father stoutly. "I sang just the way we rehearsed it. Something must have gone wrong with the microphone."

"The nerve of him!" cried another man, who must be the engineer. "Trying to put the blame on me! My microphones are perfect!"

"I'm ruined!" cried the great rock 'n' roll star. "I'll sue the station and the network and you worst of all! You've ruined my career!" He shook his fist in Abbie's father's face. "You'll hear from my lawyers in the morning." And he flounced away.

The five children looked at each other. And

while Barnaby did not say "I told you so," Abbie could tell what he was thinking and she knew that he was right. She had thwarted the magic and gone too far, and it had turned.

"I don't think the audience noticed anything," their father was saying now. "They seemed to applaud a lot. I think maybe they liked it."

"Who cares if they liked it or not?" cried the director at screamlike pitch. "*They* don't matter! You're fired and you'll never work on this program again!"

"Daddy!" Abbie couldn't help crying in tones of utter remorse at these words.

And because when magic goes wrong, it often all goes wrong at once, suddenly she and Barnaby and Fredericka and Susan and John were invisible no longer, and her father and the director and all the others looked at them and saw them.

"*You!*" cried the director, making as if to tear his hair, only he had little to tear, being bald for the most part. He turned on Abbie's father again. "Are those *your* kids? This is the last straw! You smuggle your kids in here and ruin the rehearsal, and then you sing in the wrong place and spoil the show! I'll see that you never work on *any* television network again!"

He went storming off into the wings, and his

followers followed him. And now most of the other singers and actors crowded round Abbie's father and patted him on the back and asked him sympathetically what had happened.

"I don't know," he said miserably. "I swear I wasn't wrong, but I guess I must have been."

The other actors departed, shaking their heads and looking sorry, which showed that their father was as well liked at work as he was at home. But Abbie paid small heed to this small comfort. She was clutching the book hard and pleading with it silently in her mind.

Maybe it would relent and they would find themselves back home at the same time it had been when they left, and they could spend the rest of the day right up till showtime wheedling the book and flattering it, and maybe it would unmake the magic and not let the awful thing happen.

But it didn't. She and Barnaby and the others stayed right where they were, and the awful thing was true.

Their father looked up and gave them a shaky smile.

"Hi, kids," he said. "How did you get here?"

Abbie opened her mouth but no words came out.

"We wanted to watch you rehearsing," said Barnaby, "so we clubbed together and came in on the express." Which after all was nearly the truth, for the magic had certainly been quicker than any local. "I'm sorry, Dad," he said. "I guess we all are."

But his father didn't scold them one bit, which somehow made it worse. "That's all right," he said. "If you wanted to watch me work, it's probably a good thing you came today. It may be the last chance you'll ever get. Did you buy roundtrips?"

"No," said Barnaby truthfully.

"Can you take us home?" said John. "I'll mow lawns all week and pay you back." For if Barnaby's father was out of a job, every penny would count.

"So will I," said Barnaby, who hated mowing lawns above all things.

His father took out his commutation railroad ticket and looked at it. "Six rides left," he said. "That'll use *that* up. The way things look, maybe I won't have to buy another."

Then he seemed to decide that this was self-pitying and unworthy talk. Making a comic face, he threw an arm round Fredericka and an arm round Abbie and grinned at the other three. "Come along," he said. "Home's the best place at a time like this."

Abbie could not repress a sniff, and he gave her a special smile.

"Cheer up," he said. "It's not *your* fault."

And of course it *was*, but she could never tell him so because he would never believe it.

Perhaps it would be best to draw a veil over the five children's homeward journey and the rest of the evening that followed.

Except to say that Abbie's father smiled and made jokes and tried to entertain them all the way home, which brought Abbie nearer to crying than ever, and yet she couldn't because if her father was wearing a smile to hide a breaking heart, surely the least she could do was do likewise.

And to say that when Susan and John reached Miss Centennial Peterson's house, Miss Centennial and Grannie were deep in a game of two-handed pinochle and hadn't worried or noticed how late it was at all.

When Abbie was finally alone in her own room and could cry without upsetting her father, she found that her thoughts lay too deep for tears and all she could do was think them.

Presently Barnaby stole in and sat on the foot of her bed in the dark. (Fredericka was young and heartless enough to be already asleep.)

"Don't feel too bad," he whispered. "I'd have done the same thing if I'd thought of it. You meant it for the best."

"That's no excuse," Abbie whispered back. "Who *doesn't* mean things for the best? It's the way the things work out that counts. I should have thought."

"I've been thinking now," Barnaby told her. "You keep the book tomorrow and keep on wishing. I'm willing to give up my turn and not have any wish at all, and I think John will be, too. That ought to be enough extra magic left over to fix even this up."

"Thanks," said Abbie.

When he went away, she felt a little better but not better enough. She could hear her father and mother still talking downstairs about what they would do now and how they would make ends meet. After a while she went into the hall and sat on the top step and listened.

"We'll get along," her mother was saying. "Don't worry."

"I won't," said her father, but his voice said that he was.

There was a silence.

"I nearly died when you sang out of turn," her mother said. "But it was good to hear you singing alone again." Then she chuckled. "And it *was* funny. You should have seen the expression on your face."

Her father laughed, too, and Abbie felt warm inside. That was the kind of people her mother and father were, people who could still laugh when life looked darkest. That was why she was sure they'd come out all right in the end, no matter how poor.

But she would do all she could to help. And she went back into her own room and begged the book to show its nicer side with her last waking thought.

The next morning she woke early, but Barnaby was up and dressed before her. He and Fredericka came running into Abbie's room and handed her the morning paper, folded back at the radio and television page.

"Read that," said Barnaby, pointing at a paragraph in the critic's column.

Abbie read:

"Amid the welter of trite-and-true clichés one charming moment occurred when a member of the singing group suddenly trolled forth an absurd solo at the wrong moment. The look of comic surprise on the face of the singer nearly convinced this reviewer that the carefully rehearsed episode was truly spontaneous."

"What does all that mean?" she wondered.

"It means," said Barnaby, "that he liked it."

"Oh," said Abbie. "Thanks," she added to the book. And she fetched her manicure scissors and cut the clipping out, with a scalloped edge, and put it on the tray with the breakfast that she and Barnaby and Fredericka now prepared and served their father and mother in bed.

"Well," said their father when he had read the clipping, "that's something to put in my scrapbook, anyway."

"Will it make a difference, Roy?" asked their mother.

"I shouldn't think so. I doubt if that director can read. And now," and he attacked his breakfast, "this is what I call luxury. I've been wanting a vacation for years. After we finish this elegant collation, who's for a picnic at Candlewood Lake? You," he told their mother, "are staying home from the office today."

"Roy, I can't afford to," said their mother. "And are you sure we can spare the gas?"

"We aren't going to have any talk like that," said their father. "It's not pretty talk. I'll find some kind of job next week, but right now I'm going to get to know my family. I think they're worth it."

"Can Susan and John come, too?" said Fredericka. "And Grannie?"

"Why not?" said their father. "They seem to be part of the family, too." And an hour later the little car left the driveway with eight people crammed into it somehow.

Candlewood Lake proved all that could be desired, and fish were caught and swimming prevailed and Grannie found what she was sure was a copperhead snake and quelled it with her stern pioneer gaze, so that it slunk away. And altogether no one brooded upon the dead past or thought about last night at all, except that Abbie took the book along with her and ever and anon threw it a meaningful glance.

It was nearly dinnertime when the happy voyagers arrived back at the little white house, and the phone was ringing as they turned into the driveway. Abbie and Barnaby and Fredericka's father ran to answer it at the extension on the porch. Whoever was calling seemed to be talking a blue streak, for their father kept listening and listening and saying nothing but an occasional "Oh," while his face grew more and more surprised every minute. When he finally hung up, he seemed incapable of speech, but merely stared round at them all with an expression of utter stupefaction.

"What was it?" said their mother.

"It's that director. He said they'd been trying to reach me all day. It seems that I was the hit of the show. It seems every critic on every paper said the same thing, and people have been phoning the studio and some even sent telegrams. They want me to let bygones be bygones and come back at twice the salary, and they want to feature me by name as guest star next week and have me sing 'Chickadee Tidbits' all over again. Only the songwriters are turning it into a whole big number."

"What did you say?" said their mother.

"I told him I would," said their father. "Only first I made him admit I didn't make a mistake last night."

"Then everything's going to be all right after all?" said Abbie. And she clasped the book to her breast.

"Of course it won't last," said her father. "Crazy novelties like this never do. But we ought to make a little money while it does."

"Maybe enough to buy that house over in Silvermine that I was telling you about," said their mother. "The one that's a bargain and really big enough."

And then the telephone rang again. It kept on ringing even after dinner. Sometimes it was long distance and sometimes it was telegrams. The Ed Sullivan Show wanted the children's father to be a guest and sing "Chickadee Tidbits." So did the Garry Moore Show and the Perry Como one. A record company wanted him to make a record of "Chickadee Tidbits" right away.

"They say it'll be the biggest thing since 'Mairzy Doats,' " said Abbie's father, in rather a peculiar voice.

"What's the matter?" said Abbie, who happened to be alone in the room with him at the moment.

"Oh, nothing. It's just, I never minded singing trash when I was one of a group. I had to be a good musician to do that, and the harmony made the words sound better. But for a grown man to stand up all by himself in front of a lot of other grown-up people singing,

> 'Chickadee tidbit, chickadee tidbit,
> Skedaddle skedaddle pow!'

for a living all the rest of his days. . . . Well, when I was young and hopeful and went to the Conservatory, I never thought I'd finally go down in history quite that way, that's all. Not that I'm not grateful."

The telephone rang again.

"What was it?" said Abbie when her father had hung up, his expression more peculiar than ever.

"It was the songwriters from the show. They've written me a new song they want me to introduce after I've sung 'Chickadee Tidbits' a few more times. They even sang it to me over the phone."

"How does it go?" said Abbie.

"It goes,

'Picallili kumquat, picalilli kumquat,
    Pedunkle pedunkle eek!' "

said her father.

He caught Abbie's eye. And they both started to laugh.

But that night in bed Abbie thought serious thoughts. When she found she was still thinking them in the morning, she left the house before any of the others were up and went for a walk. And she took the book with her. After all, Barnaby and John had given up their wishes and wouldn't be needing the magic. But maybe she would.

As she walked, she thought about her father and about the wish. Lots of good things were going to happen, in a money way, because of it. And yet Abbie wondered if her father were really going to be as happy as he'd been before she made it.

She had heard of a thing called human dignity, and it seemed to her that her father had always had quite a lot of this, small-part singer or not and too short or not. Something told her that he would always go on having it, but something also told her that singing,

"Chickadee tidbit, chickadee tidbit,
    Skedaddle skedaddle pow!"

for a living was going to make it harder for him to keep a firm hold on it.

She thought maybe if she could make a poem about this and tell it to the book, the book might know the answer.

Abbie was a poet who had not made many poems, as yet. The thoughts were there in her mind, but so far she could rarely bring them out of it and onto the paper. A line or two would usually come, and sometimes a whole verse, but that would be all.

There was a particular deserted woods down the road, where she liked to go to think out her poems. There was a sunny clearing at the near end of the woods and a rocky glen beyond, and if she couldn't find a line or two in the one place, she usually could in the other.

Today she perched on a log at the edge of the clearing (for the grass was still dewy), took out the pencil and paper she had brought along with the book, and wrote down,

"Alas, for human dignity!"

Then she sat and looked at the sun climbing higher in the sky and a brown butterfly on some orange butterfly weed and two towhees that were darting near her and shrieking far too loudly (for their nest was nearby and they thought the poem was a magic spell to blight their offspring, only Abbie did not know this), and no words came. Her thought was perfectly clear, but it wouldn't take shape. So she decided to try the rocky glen instead.

There was a big rock at the top of the glen where you could sit and look far down at the little stream below, where bloodroot grew in spring and cardinal flowers in summer, all among the dappled shade. It was a place for thinking vast thoughts.

But today as Abbie approached the rock, she saw that a man was already sitting there. Furthermore, the man had a pencil and paper and was writing. Quite a coincidence, thought Abbie, as she drew nearer. The man was so intent on his work that he didn't look up, even when she came quite near. He was small and untidy, with rather wild gray hair and large horn-rimmed spectacles, and altogether he looked like nothing so much as the pictures of writers you sometimes see on the covers of books. This gave Abbie courage.

"Are you an author?" she said suddenly. She had never met a real one.

The man peered at her nearsightedly over his spectacles. "More or less," he said. "I'm a poet," he added rather apologetically. "Does that count?"

"Why, so am I!" said Abbie, delighted.

"Good," said the man, and went on writing. But he didn't seem to mind Abbie's being there; so she sat beside him on the rock, as one author by another.

"Do you *finish* many poems?" she asked after a bit.

"Yes," said the man, "I do."

"I don't," said Abbie.

"You will," said the man, "if you keep trying."

There was another pause. And since her own poem didn't seem to be getting any further, Abbie looked idly at what the man was writing.

"That's not a poem," she said, "is it?"

The man looked at her. "What makes you think so?"

"It doesn't rhyme," said Abbie. "And the lines are all different lengths."

"It's a play," said the man. "It's my first play. But it's a poem, in a way. It's an opera in a way, too. At least part of it has to be sung. That's what makes it so hard."

"To finish?" said Abbie.

"*No*," said the man rather defensively. "It *is* finished. I'm just polishing. No, I mean that's what makes it so hard, getting it on the stage."

Abbie nodded wisely. In her experience of the entertainment business, hopes were often blasted.

"You mean nobody'll want to put on a play like that."

"Oh, it'll be put on all right. You see," and again he looked rather apologetic, "I happened to win a poetry prize a few years back. And a man came to me and said if I'd write a play, he'd produce it, no matter what it was. I think he's crazy, myself. It won't make a penny. Probably won't run three weeks."

"What's it about?" said Abbie.

"That's a good question," said the man. "You might say it's about modern times and what's wrong with them. Or you might say it's about a nice little man who's lost in a world of bombs and advertising and big business, and yet he won't give up. Or you might say it's about human dignity."

"*Really?*" Abbie beamed at him. "This *is* a coincidence. That's what *my* poem's about, too!"

"It is?" said the man, looking at her with new interest.

"I think it sounds like a wonderful play," said Abbie. "I don't see what you're worried about."

"Finding the right man to play the part, for one thing," said the man.

"You want some big star, I suppose," said Abbie.

"No, that's just what I *don't* want. I want somebody who's good, but people don't know about him yet. I've been looking at actors and listening to singers till I'm sick of the thought of them. I've even suffered through television shows. I saw a little man the other night who might almost do. He had the voice for it and the right face, too. Friendly-looking and lost and puzzled."

Abbie had an exciting thought. "Was he singing 'Chickadee Tidbits'?"

"Some trash or other. I even thought of finding out his name and sending him the play to read. But he probably wouldn't understand a word of it. Probably just another mindless idiot."

There was a silence. Abbie could hardly trust herself to speak. Finally she said, "Will you do me a favor?"

The interest went out of the man's face, and he looked tired and cross. "No," he said, "if you mean will I read your poem for you and tell you how to finish it, I will *not*. Students always ask me that, and it's something you have to figure out for yourself."

Abbie forgot her father and "Chickadee Tidbits" and everything else but her own outraged artistic feelings. "Of *course* I didn't mean that! I wouldn't let anyone else *touch* my poems or even look at them!"

It was the man's turn to be silent. When he

spoke, his voice was gentle. "That shows you're a true poet," he said, "and I apologize. I see I misjudged you. Why not show you forgive me by making an exception and letting me see your beginning? Since we're working on the same theme?"

With many misgivings Abbie handed him her sheet of paper.

" 'Alas for human dignity,' "

he read. He seemed to think for a minute. Then he handed the paper back.

"That's a very good first line," he said. "In fact, it's so good that I wouldn't try to do anything more with it now. Put it away and take it out every year or so and look at it. Some year you'll know what to say, and then you'll have a poem. And now, what was the favor you were going to ask me?"

"If it isn't too much trouble," said Abbie, "will you walk me home? I want you to meet my father."

Later that morning Abbie left her father and the famous man (for that is what he was and her father had recognized him right away) talking to each other in the living room and went out on the lawn, where Barnaby and John and Susan and Fredericka lay idly chatting.

"You've still got the book," said John, seeing it in her hands. "I suppose we might as well take it back to the library, since the magic's all finished."

"Is it?" said Abbie.

"Barnaby said would I give up my wish," said John, "and I said I would, and I guess it worked. Your father's going to be famous, singing 'Chickadee Tidbits,' and that's a pretty good happy ending. Nothing more'll happen now."

"Won't it?" said Abbie.

"Only let's not walk to the library just yet," said Fredericka. "It's too hot." For the fresh promise of the morning had turned to blaze and humidity, as too often happens in June.

"Who's the man with Father?" said Barnaby. "What are they doing?"

"I think they're talking business," said Abbie. She sat down and pulled up a blade of grass to nibble at the juicy white part. "Daddy'll prob'ly tell you all about it."

At that moment her father and the famous man came out on the porch.

"I still say you ought to think twice," the famous man was saying. "It'll be hard work, and it won't make you rich. You'd do far better with that 'Chickabiddy Itch,' or whatever it was."

"Let's forget about that," said Abbie's father.

"And I don't mind how hard it is. It'll be an honor to work with you, sir."

And they shook hands.

The famous man started down the walk and stopped near Abbie. "That's a good father you've got there," he said. "And *you*"—he turned back to the porch—"have quite a daughter."

"I know it," said Abbie and her father at the same time.

"We shall meet again," said the famous man. And he walked away up the road.

Abbie's father came to her and stood looking down. And in spite of the mystified others, for a minute it was as if he and she were alone together on the lawn.

"I wonder if you know what you've done for me," he said. "You've brought me the biggest chance of my life, just when I thought it was too late. Do you know that man's probably the greatest living poet in this country?"

"No, I didn't," said Abbie. But looking back, she wasn't surprised. "He's awfully understanding," she said.

She remembered wonderingly that the greatest living poet in the country had said her first line was a good one. With a shiver of joy and awe in her heart, she promised herself that she would do just as the great man had said and think about human dignity every so often, and when she finally had a poem, she would show it to him again, if they were still friends. And she felt somehow that they might still be.

But first, she would show it to her father.

Right now her father was staring at the playscript he held in his hands. "I can't believe it yet," he said. "How did it happen? How did you find him?"

Abbie thought of all the things that had happened since the day before yesterday that she could never tell him because there were no words for some of them and the rest he wouldn't believe.

Then she looked around at the others and winked.

"I made a wish," she said.

Keeping It?

That night after dinner Abbie's father read the play out loud to the whole family, and to John and Susan because they asked to be included.

Parts of it were exciting, and parts were so funny that Abbie's father could hardly read for laughing. Other parts were hard for the children to follow (though Barnaby claimed he understood every word), but the poetry was so beautiful that Abbie felt humble. When she said as much, her father admitted to feeling humble, too, at the thought of acting a character that was so long and complicated and demanding and rewarding.

"Are you sure you ought to do it, Roy?" Abbie's mother wondered.

"I'm sure," said Abbie's father, "that I ought to try."

And then everyone separated for bed.

But for the third night that week, Barnaby came

tiptoeing into Abbie's room, after all the lights were out.

"I've been thinking," he said. "I promised to give up my wish if it'd help Father, and so did John. But how can we be sure we have to now? It was *your* wish that made that poet turn up. Maybe he'd have come along anyway if John and I hadn't promised a thing. I don't think it'd do any harm to test the book and see if there's still some magic left."

"Maybe not," said Abbie. But when Barnaby had departed for his own room, she lay waking and doubtful. It seemed suspiciously like double-dealing to her. Still, who was she to say so? She had *had* her wish, and it had turned out in the end to be the best wish of all.

And Barnaby hadn't had a turn but had been having ideas and helping the others, from the beginning. Who could blame him for wanting a wish of his own before all magic failed?

Meanwhile, in the house across the street, John was having the same thought. But because his mind worked more slowly than Barnaby's, light didn't fully dawn until breakfast-time next morning. When it did, he hustled Susan through her oatmeal and across the street, where Barnaby and Abbie and Fredericka were weeding the petunia bed, which was their morning chore.

Many hands made light work, and soon the petunias were free of the sourgrass and plantains that had gotten into the bed with them, and the five children sought the shade.

"Now," said Barnaby, and he and John started talking, both at once, each explaining his own idea. But since their ideas were exactly the same, the general sense came through.

"How about it?" said Barnaby finally. "Shall we have a try?"

"Why not?" said Fredericka.

Abbie said nothing, but she felt troubled.

As for Susan, she was only half listening as she idly glanced through the book, reviewing its colorful descriptions of their adventures in the past. Now she closed the cover, but it fell open again at the back flyleaf, and something caught her eye. She looked closer. Then she looked up.

"We can't," she said. "You forgot. So did I. It's a seven-day book, and today's Saturday. It's due back at the library right now."

"Then the magic's over," said Abbie.

"Not necessarily," said Barnaby. "I could have my wish, and *then* we could take it back. It'd still be today."

"What about me?" said John.

"I was forgetting," said Barnaby.

"I wasn't," said John. "I could have my wish, *too*, and then we could take it back."

"Two wishes in the same day?" Susan was doubtful. "It might be awfully hard on it."

Barnaby had an idea. "Or even better," he said excitedly, "why take it back at all? Till we're good and ready, I mean. We've kept books out overtime before this when they were due and we hadn't finished with them. We could club together and pay the fine!"

Susan still looked doubtful, and Abbie thought it was time to speak.

"It'd be wrong," she said regretfully. "I *know* it would. It'd be breaking the rules of the magic, and you know what happens when somebody does *that*!"

"That's usually the most exciting part," said Fredericka. "*Let's!*"

"Three against two," said Barnaby. "That's fair enough."

He looked at Abbie. But what could Abbie say?

"All right, then," he went on. "We win. The book stays out till we're through with it. You won't mind if I have my turn today, will you, old man? You can have yours tomorrow. I know just what I'm going to wish."

"Yes, I *do* mind," said John with unwonted stubbornness. "I know just what *I'm* going to wish, *too*."

"Later," said Barnaby, reaching for the book. But John got in his way.

"Your family's had the book for the past three days," he said. "It's time *we* had a chance. Besides, I'm oldest."

"But wait till you hear what my wish *is*," said Barnaby.

"I don't want to," said John. "You're always so sure your ideas are best. Well, maybe somebody else can have an idea for a change!"

Abbie looked worriedly from one to the other. "It's all going wrong," she said. "It started the minute you said you'd keep the book. Let's change our minds before you start fighting. Remember last time!"

Once in the past John and Barnaby had had a fight, and it had been awful, maybe because they were usually best friends, and when best friends fall out, it is worse than any other quarrel. All their regard for each other seems to sour and turn to spite and meanness. And the hurts that friends can do each other cut deeper and take longer to heal.

Right now John and Barnaby were eyeing each other in a way that reminded Abbie of that other awful time. John's face was red and his forehead creased in an ugly frown. Barnaby was pale and he was smiling, but it was a dangerous smile.

"You couldn't have an idea like this one," he said tauntingly, "in a million years."

"That's the worst of you little runts," said John, "always boasting 'cause you're too weak to do anything else!"

"Little" is a fighting word, and so is "runt," and "weak" is unforgivable. To hear them all in one sentence was too much for Barnaby, and his smile seemed to freeze on his face. "Oh, can't I?" he said. "Where's that book?"

Dodging past John, he grabbed it rather roughly from Susan's hand.

"You can't push *my* sister around!" cried John.

"He didn't," said Susan mildly, but John was past heeding.

"You give that back," he said, and he, too, laid hold of the book.

"Stop them, somebody!" wailed Abbie. "Let's take the book back to the library right now, before it's too late!"

But it already was.

The tug of war the book was undergoing proved too much for its age-worn spine. Suddenly it gave way, and John was left clutching a few torn-out pages while Barnaby waved the rest of the book triumphantly before his eyes.

"Just for that," he cried, "I'm going alone. I don't need *any* of you! Good-bye!"

And he was gone.

John looked stupidly from the place where Barnaby had been standing to the piece of book in his hand. His face was pale now and not angry at all. "Gee," he said. "I didn't mean *that* to happen. Why'd I get so mad?"

"It's the magic," said Abbie. "It *wants* to go back to the library. When you said it couldn't, it made you get all horrible."

"I know," said John, shamefaced. "I could hear myself being awful, but I couldn't stop. I'm sorry." He looked at the torn pages in his hand. They were blank, save for the back flyleaf of the book, from which the library slip stared up at him ironically with today's date stamped on it.

Susan saw this at the same time, and now it was her turn to utter a cry. "Oh!" she said. "You've got the *last* pages. That means Barnaby's off somewhere in the middle of some adventure with a magic book that hasn't got any ending! And *that* prob'ly means his *adventure* won't have an ending and he'll never get out of it and come home again!"

"We'd better find him right away," said John, all his anger forgotten in concern for his friend. "Where would he be?"

"Somewhere in some book," said Fredericka. "Trust Barnaby!" But her smile was a shaky one.

As for Abbie, she was near tears, but she forced her mind to think. "Maybe *Robinson Crusoe*," she ventured. "One whole year he hardly read anything else."

"Well," said John, "here goes. I hope."

Everyone joined hands, and he wished on the tattered remnant of magic that was all they had left. And perhaps because the end of a book is its most important part in a way and a key to all that has gone before, the magic worked as well as if its outward and visible form hadn't been mutilated at all. The next instant the four children found themselves standing on a rocky and beach-rimmed isle by a blue and sounding sea under a hot and cloudless sky.

In the distance a familiar figure was silhouetted against the horizon. It wore a jacket and cap of goatskin and carried an umbrella of the same material. Following it at a respectful distance was another figure, of native aspect. Otherwise, and in every direction, the island was plainly uninhabited. As Fredericka said afterwards, desert was putting it mildly. And the only extra footprints on the sand were the four children's own.

"He isn't here," said Susan.

"Unless he's turned *into* one of them," said Ab-

1 6 5

bie, pointing at the distant figures. But this was plainly nonsense. Robinson Crusoe and Friday are Robinson Crusoe and Friday forever and ever, and *no one* could take their place, magic or not.

"Where'll we try next?" said John. "What's he been reading lately?"

"Dickens," said Fredericka. "Ever since we saw that old movie of *David Copperfield* on television, he's been working his way through our set of Complete Works. He says they're worth it. I say they're too long. Too sad, too."

"We might as well try everything," said John. Once more the four children joined hands. But first they rubbed their footprints out carefully so Robinson and Friday wouldn't think ghosts had been visiting their beach. And *then* John wished.

It was quite a change from the island's tropic glare to Christmas Eve in old London. The children's breath smoked on the chilly air, and a few snowflakes fell. Chimes rang and carol-singers sang carols.

"Humbug!" muttered an old gentleman, emerging from his office. But "Merry Christmas!" said almost everyone to almost everyone else.

A ragged boy who was sweeping the street crossing didn't seem merry at all, however, and Abbie, touched by his poor and friendless looks, pressed her only nickel into his hand, hoping he could later exchange it for coinage of the realm at the nearest bank.

"Move on," said a passing policeman.

The boy moved on, and Abbie ran to join the others, who were looking in at a window of one of the houses.

Inside the window a poor but happy family was finishing its Christmas pudding and drawing round the hearth, where chestnuts sputtered and cracked, while the father of the family poured holiday drinks from a jug.

"God bless us every one," said the crippled son of the family, raising his custard cup (without a handle).

But Barnaby was not among those at Tiny Tim's Christmas dinner.

Inside the Old Curiosity Shop across the street, where the four children ran to look next, Little Nell and her grandfather were hopefully packing for their long, wandering journey into the country.

But Barnaby was not among the other curiosities in the shop.

"This is no good," said John. "That Dickens wrote about seventy books, didn't he? We'll never find the right one this way."

"And maybe the right one isn't Dickens at all," said Abbie.

"We need a system," said John.

"Well," said Fredericka, "there's that bookshelf at home by Barnaby's bed where he keeps all his favorite ones."

"Why, yes," said Abbie. "We could go home and make a list and then try them all one by one."

"Reading from left to right," put in Susan, who liked things to be methodical.

John shook his head. "*Our* book wouldn't stand it," he said. "It'd wear out." And indeed the few pages in his hand were already looking weather-beaten, what with exposure to the tropic sun followed suddenly by snowflakes melting all over them. "Besides, think of all the *other* books he's read from the library. He could be in any one of them. And he's taken out hundreds more than any of us. Lots that we've prob'ly never heard of, even!"

"Wait," said Abbie, for these words had given her an idea. But it needed thinking out, and maybe she would be betraying a secret.

"You remember," she began slowly, "that book of his own that he's working on?"

"Is there really one?" said John. The others had heard of Barnaby's book, but they'd never given it much thought. Probably it was just another of his ideas.

"Yes, there really is," said Abbie. "At least he

has these adventures he makes up when he can't sleep, and he's put some of them down on paper. Well, I was thinking, if you were mad at people and running away from them, wouldn't a story of your own be just the place you'd go and hide in?"

"What's his story about?" said John.

"He wouldn't ever tell me very much," said Abbie. "All I know is, he calls it 'Barnaby the Wanderer,' and it's about this boy sort of like *him*, except he goes wandering around on his own having adventures all by himself. So you see the being alone part works out, too."

"Where does he wander?" said Fredericka.

"Just about everywhere, I guess. All over the world, and I know he goes into the past, but not the future, because Barnaby said once he hasn't worked that part out yet."

"That's something," said John. "That narrows it down. He's somewhere in the present or the past, and he's somewhere in some country."

"*Our* book'll know," said Abbie. "Just wish to be with him and let the magic figure out where."

"But would our book know about a book that's not finished yet, and it's still just in somebody's mind?" said Susan.

"I think," said Abbie, "that our book would know about *everything*."

"Let's try," said Fredericka.

For the third time the four children joined hands and for a third time John wished.

"We want to go after Barnaby the Wanderer," he told the magic, "wherever he's wandering."

And the magic took them there.

Barnaby the Wanderer wandered along the road.

It was a good road to wander along because *it* wandered, *too*, all over the map and in and out of the centuries. Today, for example, when he went through that last valley, it had been Old Roman times, but now that he was climbing the hill, it was Merrie England and the Ages were Middle.

He had been delayed a little in the valley because Julius Caesar was conquering Gaul down there at the moment, and the leader of one of his cohorts had suddenly developed the falling sickness, and Barnaby the Wanderer had to step in and save the day. When the battle was over and won, Caesar wanted him to join the army and be second in command. But Barnaby the Wanderer would never stay, no matter how hard people begged. Always he must wander on.

Right now he wandered up the hill into the Age of Chivalry. He could tell it was the Age of Chivalry because of all the castles scattered here and there about the landscape and all the knights he could see riding in different directions on different quests. But Barnaby the Wanderer was the most gallant knight among them. And soon he had a chance to prove it.

As he reached the crest of the hill, a lady galloped toward him on a palfrey, closely pursued by a giant on a black steed. Barnaby the Wanderer knew the giant well by sight. He was a particularly mean specimen who made a habit of kidnapping ladies and taking them to a dolorous tower, where he married them and treated them in a Bluebeard manner. But this time he had met his match.

Barnaby the Wanderer drew his lance and barred the way.

"Oh gramercy," remarked the lady, reining in her horse and preparing to watch the combat with interest.

"Out of the way, minikin," said the giant rudely, sneering down at Barnaby the Wanderer from his vast height. "Your puny lance would be but a mere pinprick to such as me! Besides, you're too short to reach! Yah!"

Barnaby the Wanderer wasted no breath in answering back. His strength was as the strength of ten because he was Barnaby the Wanderer. With a mighty heave he sent his lance vaulting into the air.

Its point entered the giant's throat in the space between helmet and breastplate, and he toppled from
the saddle and crashed to the ground. Barnaby the
Wanderer whipped out his sword and wapped off
the giant's head, thus rendering him harmless.

"Oh, thank you!" cried the lady. "Did you do
this for love of me?"

"No, I didn't," said Barnaby the Wanderer. "I
did it to show I could and because he thoroughly
deserved it." And mounting the giant's horse he rode
off into the sunset.

"Stay with me," called the lady after him in
languishing tones.

But Barnaby the Wanderer would never stay.
He had a rendezvous with destiny.

As he rode on, though, he rather wished he had
someone with him to talk to and maybe boast a little
about recent events. He remembered some friends
he used to have, in another time and country, and
wondered what they were doing now. Probably they
were wondering and worrying about *him*. Very well,
let them wonder. He must follow his fate alone.

At this moment the sun went behind a cloud
and a mist rose from the earth.

"This is unusual," thought Barnaby the Wanderer. "For me the sun shines always fair."

But this time it didn't. The mist grew until it

mantled the entire landscape. Trees turned to huddled shapes, and who could say where was land and
where was air? Suddenly the horse shied and would
go no farther, but stood shivering and staring into
the blankness with the rolling eye of fright.

Barnaby the Wanderer dismounted and tied the
horse's reins to a bush. At least it *looked* like a bush
and *felt* like a bush, but what with the mist growing
ever thicker it might have been something else.

"Where am I?" thought Barnaby the Wanderer.

But he wandered on, leaving the horse snorting
with fear behind him. Nothing must keep him from
his chosen road. Besides, what with the mist now
eddying and wreathing in tendrils about him and
seeming to cling to his clothes and trying to hold
him back, he could see better on foot and closer to
the ground. But he wished he had not chosen to
walk alone, just this once. He thought of friends
left behind and wished one or all of them were with
him now. No matter. He would show them. Or if he
never returned, they would be sorry when he was
gone.

What made the mist nastier than most mists was
that it seemed to have a voice, or voices.

"Hist," whispered the mist.

Barnaby the Wanderer stood still.

"List," whispered the mist.

Barnaby the Wanderer listened.

"Listen, listen, do not hasten.
  Enter not the Western postern
  Where the ghastly cistern glistens,
  Lest you learn the last, worst lesson,"

whispered the mist.

"Humph!" said Barnaby the Wanderer aloud. "No mere mist can mistlead *me*. I am Barnaby the Wanderer!"

"Mere, mere, mirror!" shrieked a sudden voice in his ear, followed by a peal of witchlike laughter.

"Ponder the pun," added a quieter voice in his other ear. But when he reached out his hand, there was no one there.

Still, he knew where he was now, or thought he did. He was in a time that never was on land or sea, in that Grimm, Thurber-ish country where witches are worse than ever was in Oz, and there are gloomy castles with thirteen clocks all stopped, and a Todal that gleeps and a Golux that harkens and warns.

He thought of other creepy legends, of the headless horseman of Sleepy Hollow and the Come-at-a-body that has more legs than arms and more hair than either. And he thought that this was not a time or a place to be alone in.

Still, all the more glory to him who explored it and lived to tell the tale, thought Barnaby the Wanderer on second thought. And he took out his pocket compass, though he could hardly see it through the moist mist, and turned toward the west.

As he stepped westward, the mist seemed to thin, and ahead the land was bright. Suddenly the foggy, dewy strands fell away, and his heart lifted as he emerged into a sun-drenched clearing. Straight before him was a gate, flanked on either side by a tall thorn hedge.

When Barnaby the Wanderer had last seen the sun, it was setting, but now it shone at high noon. Perhaps in this part of the country they had Daylight Saving, he thought. Or more likely here the time stood still.

The gate was built of stone and prettily planted about with clumps of narcissi, now in full bloom and scenting the air. There were letters carved on the gate's pediment, and he wandered closer to read them.

"Abandon Hope, All Ye Who Center Here," said the letters.

Barnaby the Wanderer thought he had read this sentence before, somewhere. But he thought that whoever had carved it on the gate hadn't gotten all of the words exactly right.

He hesitated. A gate might well be a postern, and this was almost surely the Western one, and he remembered the warning words of the mist. He had no wish to abandon hope or to learn any last worst lesson, either. But he was curious to see what was inside.

Then for the first time in a long while he re-membered the magic book, which he'd put in his pocket for safekeeping, back when he was fighting the giant. He slapped his pocket to see if it was still there, and it was. Surely it would protect him. Not that he needed protecting, of course. Barnaby the Wanderer would always come out on top and without any help from anybody.

The gate was ajar, and he slipped through it.

For a moment he was disappointed at what he saw.

What he saw was a garden with a pool in the middle. And the pool didn't look like a ghastly cis-tern at all. It looked like an ordinary (though very handsome) marble pool. Probably there would be goldfish. He stepped closer to look.

There were no fish in the pool, only water, but water that was clearer and brighter than any he had ever seen before. And there, staring up from the water (and seeming to smile at him as Barnaby himself smiled in recognition) was his own reflection.

But never in any glass had he seen himself so clearly. Now for the first time he realized just how handsome and brilliant and wonderful he really was, more so even than he had always suspected.

"I am Barnaby the Wanderer!" he cried in tones of glad discovery.

And he fell on his knees by the pool to look closer.

Then as he looked the image changed.

Written in the face in the pool he suddenly seemed to see all the base, unworthy thoughts he had ever had and all the bad things he had ever done, rude, inconsiderate things and careless, forgetful things and hasty, hotheaded, spiteful things. And the face in the pool now seemed to him mean and selfish and hideous beyond belief.

He tried to tear his eyes away, but he couldn't. Something held them there. And he realized that he was under a magic spell and that the magic was stronger than he was.

In a panic he scrabbled in his pocket for the book and wished to be anywhere else in the world rather than here, but home with his family and friends would be best of all.

Nothing happened. Except that the face in the pool seemed to grow bigger and look worse.

Then he remembered that one of the bad things he had done was to tear the magic book, and now the magic had probably leaked out of it and he was probably doomed to kneel here staring at his own ugliness forever.

"I am Barnaby the Wanderer!" he cried, to reassure himself.

But that magic charm didn't work, either. And Barnaby the Wanderer knew despair.

From despair to remorse is but a step. He went over his worst deeds in his mind and regretted every one of them.

Then as the sun beat down and the face stared from the pool, all of the past seemed to blur and run together in his brain. His head ached, and even today's adventures faded and were forgotten. When he tried to think of home, he couldn't remember where he lived or the names of his sisters.

"I am Barnaby the Wanderer!" he tried to say again. But he had forgotten the right words. "I am Barnaby the Barnaby" was what came out. And after that, "Barnaby, Barnaby, Barnaby" was all he could find to say. He thought it was someone's name, but he had forgotten whose.

The magic book slipped from his fingers and fell at the edge of the water. In the pool the face seemed to swell until it filled the world and dominated the universe. Barnaby leaned closer, staring into its eyes. But he had forgotten what face it was, or why he was looking at it.

And the waters of the pool lapped nearer and nearer to the magic book.

If John had worded his wish differently, the magic might have taken the four children directly to the narcissus-y pool. But he had asked to follow Barnaby, wherever he was wandering; so now he and Susan and Abbie and Fredericka found themselves walking a winding and hilly road.

The first thing they met was the corpse of the giant. Susan and Abbie shut their eyes, but John and Fredericka surveyed it with interest.

"Pretty good," said John, "for a little fellow." And his tone made amends for the "runt" he had meanly uttered before.

"David and Goliath," agreed Fredericka, "would be putting it mildly."

The mist delayed the four children a little, but not so long as it had Barnaby, for it was not in a talking mood at the moment. The horse tied to the bush proved a puzzlement, but kind Abbie undid its reins and it galloped happily away to be a free wild horse forever.

Westward the land was brighter, and the four children turned toward it. A second later they came into the clearing. The gate stood open, and they hurried through.

They were just in time.

The lapping waters of the pool had reached the book by now, and a second later they might have carried it away, to what dark depths of oblivion who could tell?

But John ran forward and snatched it up and put his few last pages with it. And now that the book was whole again, the spell was broken, and Barnaby wrenched his eyes away from the face in the pool and turned and saw and knew them.

"You came," he said. "Thanks."

John put the two pieces of book into his hands. "Here," he said.

Barnaby looked at the book. Then he handed it back. "No," he said. His eyes were on John's. "Take it," he said. "It's all yours."

And everything between them that could never be talked about they had said in those few words.

There was a silence. Susan was watching John.

"Aren't you going to wish?" she asked. "It's your

turn now. What was that adventure *you* wanted?"

"*The Three Musketeers*," said John slowly, "but now I don't know."

"Why do we need *them*?" said Fredericka, jigging up and down on the edge of the pool. "All they'd prob'ly do would be come riding to the rescue, and we've already rescued Barnaby perfectly well by ourselves!"

"Don't!" said Barnaby, in quick alarm. "Don't boast; it's dangerous. And come away from that pool before you look in." He pulled his sister to a safe distance; then he turned back to John.

"Wish *something*," he said. "I'll feel a lot better about everything if you do."

"All right," said John. "First of all I wish we were home."

And they were.

8

Giving It Back

"And now," said John, "the next thing to do is take that book back to the library."

There was a chorus of protest from the others, sitting beside him on the steps of the big white house.

"Why?" was the general sense of everyone's remarks.

"Because I think it's time," said John.

"Without any adventure of your own? It doesn't seem right," said Susan. "In every book I ever read there was a wish for each one."

"Well," said John, "I've been thinking it over, and this is what I think. If I have a wish, then it's all sort of rounded out and the magic can end and maybe never start up again. But if I don't and we take the book back, then there's still unfinished business. And maybe someday the magic'll come back and take up where it left off."

Everyone gasped mentally at the nobility of this self-sacrifice.

"You mean we'll find the book again someday?" said Fredericka.

"That," said John, "or in some other form."

This was an exciting idea and showed definitely that Barnaby was not the only one who could have these. But Barnaby was still unhappy about the justice of it.

"I'll always think it was my fault," he said, "and it *will* be. Can you condemn a fellow human to the pangs of guilt?"

But he meant it.

"Well," said John slowly again, "I'll tell you what let's do. We'll take the book back, but we'll take it back *my way*."

"But first," said Susan, "wait till I get something."

She ran to fetch glue and Scotch tape and a needle and thread, and she and Abbie fell to mending the damage the boys had done. And the book seemed so glad to be its full self again that the paper practically leaped to meet the glue and the torn binding all but embraced the benevolent needle, till in the end you would hardly have known that the hands of wrath had ever rent the book in twain in the first place.

"Now," said John. And he wished.

"What book are we part of now?" said Abbie a few seconds later, as the five children found themselves floating through the air with the greatest of ease on newly fledged wings.

"Lots of different ones," said Barnaby. "Flying comes into just about every magic book I ever read. It's just about everybody's first wish."

Fredericka, more daring than the others, now attempted to loop the loop, but she wasn't quite used to her wings yet and lost altitude dangerously, nearly grazing the tops of some tall trees.

"Auks!" said a bird-watcher who happened to be standing below.

"Hawks?" said his wife, who was rather deaf.

"No, auks," said the man. "*Great* auks, by the size. And they're extinct, you know. I shall write to Miss Bristow's bird column."

But otherwise no one looked up and saw them all the length of lower Weed Street. It is surprising how few people *do* look up during the course of a day, though they might find it rewarding if they did.

At the corner of Weed Street and Richmond Hill, John perched in an oak tree, and the other four flocked to nearby branches, greatly to the annoyance of seven bird families of various species who were already nesting in the tree and who now all started uttering their different calls at the top of their voices, in shrill complaint at the crowded conditions.

"We change here," said John, and indeed they had, for their wings had already vanished. "I couldn't decide between wings and magic carpets; so I wished both."

At this moment their particular magic carpet arrived, right on cue, and the five children clambered on. Riding it was even more fun than flying had been, for it involved less of what tennis players call "form." All the five children had to do was sit while the carpet rose stiffly in the air and then took off at a swift horizontal. As a great writer on the subject has put it, it was like tobogganing, only there was no doormat to stop short on. (I think the great writer must have been thinking of the kind of tobogganing that is done on front staircases, with tin trays, a sport that might well be revived more generally.)

The shooting, sliding feeling went on and on without a bump, but only as far as the library roof, to which the carpet soared swift as any homing pigeon and without having to be steered at all.

"Look," said John. "No hands!"

Luckily the roof was a flat one, and the carpet paused on it long enough for the five children to

clamber off, before proceeding on its way, probably back to some Arabian night.

There was a trap door in the roof, and it was accommodatingly unlocked. Where John led, the others followed. They went down a ladder and found themselves in the upper part of the library, where they had never ventured before because only grown-ups were allowed.

On every hand were what looked like thousands of books, ranged on shelves, stacks and stacks of them.

"Think of all those that we haven't read yet!" said Abbie.

"Maybe some of them have magic inside, too!" said Fredericka.

"*All* of them, I should think," said Barnaby, "one way or another."

They went down a staircase and through a door at the bottom to the main floor, and no one noticed or questioned them. But just outside the children's room they stood hesitating.

"I hate to say good-bye," said Susan, and she voiced the thoughts of all five.

"Maybe it's just *au revoir*," said Abbie.

"If the magic ever does come back into our lives," said Barnaby to John, "you get first turn. Needless to say."

And the five children went into the children's room, Susan leading the way and carrying the book because it was she who had found it in the first place.

She thought Miss Dowitcher looked at her a bit strangely when she saw what the book was, but "Oh, that!" was all she said. "Did you enjoy it?"

"Yes," said Susan, "we did. It got a little bit torn just at the end, though."

Miss Dowitcher riffled through the back pages. "I don't see where," she said.

And neither could Susan, now. The book had grown together and was its old plump, comfortable, shabby, but untorn self again. And Susan noticed something else about it.

As Miss Dowitcher laid the book aside with other books that were to be put back on the shelves, Susan nudged Barnaby and Barnaby nudged Abbie and Abbie nudged John and John nudged Fredericka and they all looked where Susan was looking.

On the book's spine, where before the old gold lettering had been rubbed away, new letters shone.

Seven-Day Magic, the letters read.

"It's got a name now," said John.

"And we made it," said Barnaby.

"Only it doesn't say who the author is," said Susan.

"That's 'cause there wasn't room to put all of us," said Fredericka.

"I wonder who'll take it out next," said Abbie. "And will it be a magic wishing book for them, *too*, or just a book of stories about *us*?"

Miss Eulalie Smythe Prang looked up from the far end of the table where she was sitting and sighed, putting her hand to her head as if it ached.

"Please," she said. "Can't we have quiet?"

The five children went out of the library and along the village street that turned into the curving country road home.

Edward Eager (1911–1964) worked primarily as a playwright and lyricist. It wasn't until 1951, while searching for books to read to his young son, Fritz, that he began writing children's stories. In each of his books he carefully acknowledges his indebtedness to E. Nesbit, whom he considered the best children's writer of all time—"so that any child who likes my books and doesn't know hers may be led back to the master of us all."